A COMEDY SCI-FI ADVENTURE SERIES

BY

...Don't you have any Bengal matches?...

BOOK THREE - PART TWO

© TITLE FONT & ILLUSTRATION BY SAM LUCAS

OSCAR PISCINE BOOK PUBLISHING

ISBN 978-1-7398855-4-0

Paperback Version

DOWNFALL: PART TWO BY SAM LUCAS © 2022

WWW.SAMLUCASBOOKS.COM
e-mail:samlucasbooks@btinternet.com

PUBLISHER - OSCAR PISCINE BOOKS

ACT 3, SCENE 1

1.32pm, Friday 17th October, 2025. George London and his group of ex-SAS soldiers have parachuted over the Village of Tulla and landed in the nearby woods. Ahead of them, Russian soldiers armed with AK-47's patrol the Numenobman lake. Heavy machinery, trucks, amphibious tanks, combat reconnaissance patrol vehicles, jeeps and a large crane gather at the west side of the lake. Frogmen emerge from the murky water carrying pieces of alien spaceship and strange looking devices. They hand them over to soldiers in boats then disappear back under. On the surface, the lake is covered with radio valves bobbing up and down. In the afternoon sunlight, they look like tiny glass people chattering to one another. George London and his group of soldiers stealthily cover the ground to the east side of the lake and quickly set up a base camp. They are now 400 metres from the action on the west side and observe the enemy with binoculars.

LONDON
What do you make of it Cavendish?

(George London passes over

*his binoculars to ex-Staff
Sergeant Michael Cavendish.
Cavendish is a big chap from
Yorkshire and stands 6ft 6"
in his bare feet. He is 47
years old, well tanned, bald,
and has several small facial
scars.)*

CAVENDISH

Heavy artillery, tanks, Splinter MK-7's, MT-2 Lock-on Smite Retaliators, a ZX-81 Pin Wheel, a Hans-brown Grenade Propeller, a HK-8 Blade Dissector, J-45 Whizz-bangs, Rocket Launchers, Philo Plasma Liquefiers and at least 50 men with AK-47's, ZX-MF8 tactical rifles, Grad-13 Sniper rifles and what looks like a 13th Century Trebuchet.

LONDON

Haven't seen one of those in ages. Could be a bit tricky. We better observe them for a while and come up with a strategy...

*(London moves from his prone
position and sits on a fallen
log.)*

...Don't know about you, but my feet could do with a good soak, haven't worn army boots for years. Well, you keep an eye on things here and I'll

go and see if Pilky's got the tea
on...

(*London gets to his feet.*)

...Let's just hope he's remembered to
bring the Fig Rolls and the Pikelets.

(*London walks over to see
Cyril Pilkington at their
encampment. Pilkington is 72
but is often mistaken for a
child. He is a small thin
man with a gaunt complexion
and odd mannerisms. He has a
pleasant Lancastrian accent.*)

LONDON
Ah, there you are Pilky. How's it
going with the tea?

PILKINGTON
The matches are wet and the wood's
damp.

LONDON
Don't you have any Bengal matches?

PILKINGTON
No, you can't get those anymore.
Health and Safety banned them.

LONDON
What! That's disgraceful, can't

imagine a childhood without those.
Old Johnny Carstairs used to love
Bengal matches - he was always
throwing them at people; especially
loved lobbing them into the hood of a
Parker jacket...

> *(London smiles and walks
> towards Pilkington.)*

...And then he would run up to the
person and put the fire out, telling
them a story about a passing firework
display and how he'd saved them...

> *(His smile dissipates.)*

...Of course he's dead now, just like
all the good old fellows.

> *(Pilkington moves the damp
> wood around and tries to
> light it again.)*

                    PILKINGTON
How did he die?

                    LONDON
Burnt to death in a fire.

                    PILKINGTON
That's awful, how did it happen?

LONDON

Circus tent. They're quite flammable
y'know. He was performing his death-
defying act of riding a bicycle along
a tightrope while juggling with fire
sticks. In the middle of his act,
his bicycle wheel came loose and he
threw one of the sticks too high.
Unfortunately for Carstairs it got
caught in the frame work of the tent.
Of course within a few minutes the
whole place was on fire - went up
like a paint factory. Crowds of
people running everywhere; elephants,
bears, lions and clowns all in a
fluster. The whole thing was a total
disaster...

*(Pilkington pulls an
emergency flare out of his
pocket, strikes the end of it
and rams it into the fire.
Within seconds a huge fire is
throwing out heat.)*

...Ah, that's better. Well done
Pilky.

*(Cavendish runs towards
London and Pilkington,
screaming like a wild
banshee.)*

CAVENDISH

Put that fire out! Put that fire

out!

    (London and Pilkington look
stunned. Cavendish jumps
onto the fire and starts
stamping it out with his
feet.)

LONDON

I say Cavendish, poor old Pilky has
just lit that. What a rotter you
are.

CAVENDISH

Are you two stupid, why don't you
send the Russians an invitation? We
are supposed to be stealthy and
furtive, remain unseen - this is a
covert operation, not a day out at
the beach roasting marshmallows over
a fire.

    (London looks at Cavendish
with annoyance.)

LONDON

If I didn't know better Cavendish, I
would say you were questioning my
leadership skills. If we can't have
a cup of tea and a Pikelet, what's
the point. Those Russian chaps
aren't even looking this way, they're
more interested in what's at the
bottom of that lake. You could hold

a carnival over here and they
wouldn't notice.

>   (*Out of the woods, twenty*
>   *Russian soldiers armed with*
>   *rifles appear from nowhere*
>   *and confront London and his*
>   *team of ex-SAS.*)

                    RUSSIAN SERGEANT
Arms up?

>   (*Cavendish looks at London.*)

                    CAVENDISH
A carnival, what a plonker.

                    LONDON
I say Cavendish, I didn't know you
were such a stinker.

                    RUSSIAN SERGEANT
Stop talking.

                    RUSSIAN PRIVATE
What shall we do with them?

                    RUSSIAN SERGEANT
Take them back to the camp...

>   (*The Russian sergeant looks*
>   *at his men.*)

...Private Petrov, Sokolov and Volkov. You stay here with me to help search their equipment. The rest of you get going.

(*London and his group of ex-SAS soldiers are lead away from their encampment and head for the west side of the lake.*)

LONDON
Don't worry chaps, this is just a temporary setback, I'm sure the Russians will have some tea. Pity about those Pikelets, but I believe the Russians do a version of a Mille-feullie called Napoleon cake. If I remember correctly, it was something to do with defeating the French.

Scene fades.

ACT 3, SCENE 2

On planet EgÁs, the afternoon wears on
and the workers have erected tents,
dug latrines and mapped out the foot
of Ra-eb's Claw with twine and stakes.
Tac is busy talking with Sir Daot and
an agreement on where to start digging
is the main topic of conversation. He
holds a map in his hands and points to
various locations.

TAC

...Well, the men have mapped out
sector F to sector P. I think that's
our best bet to find an underground
entrance. I have made a detailed
survey of the area and believe Sector
K to be the best place to start
digging, and then work out from there
a section at a time.

SIR GORF DAOT

Yes, well you seem to know what you
are doing. Glad to have you here,
we'd be lost without you.

(Eeb appears from behind a
rock.)

EEB

Sir, come quickly. We've found
something, an entrance with some
steps.

                    TAC
What are you talking about Eeb, we
haven't even started digging yet.

                    EEB
Not on your sector, no, we're still
putting down the string on your bit
boyo. This was over the other side
of the camp, a hundred yards away.

                    TAC
What are you doing over there? No
one authorised you to dig in that
location.

                    EEB
Yes they did.

                    TAC
Who?

                    EEB
You did. You told me to get some men
and go and dig a latrine a hundred
yards away from the camp; and you
pointed over there...

    (Eeb points into the desert.)

...And that's what I did. Nelson and
MacTavish are over there now. Fairly
uncovered a lot of sand they have...

    (Eeb is still pointing into

the desert.)

...Do you want to have a look, or
shall I tell Nelson and MacTavish to
fill it back up like?

                    TAC
Well, I suppose we ought to have a
look, but it seems a waste of time,
especially when we've mapped out this
area. Are you up for a walk Sir
Daot?

                SIR GORF DAOT
Erm, thought I might have a bit of a
rest actually, touch of sciatica
playing up. You go and have a look
and let me know if you find anything
of interest.

        *(Tac and Eeb walk over to the
        latrine. Nelson and
        MacTavish are nowhere to be
        seen. Stone steps leading
        into a big hole head
        underground and out of
        sight.)*

                    EEB
See, what did I tell you boyo.

                    TAC
Certainly looks promising. Fetch us
some torches and we'll go and see...

(Eeb runs off to go and get some torches and leaves Tac by the hole. After a few minutes, curiosity wins him over and he enters the hole holding his cigarette lighter.)

...Looks pretty deep!

(After running around the encampment for some torches, Eeb returns to the hole successful.)

                    EEB
Are you there boyo?

(Eeb stands at the entrance to the hole, holding two torches.)

                    TAC
I'm down here. Bring the torches...

(Eeb lights the torches with a match and walks down the steps. After a few minutes he sees Tac. Tac is standing next to a wall holding his lighter up to some hieroglyphs.)

...Ah, good. Look at this Eeb, fascinating.

*(Eeb hands Tac one of the
torches and the area comes to
life.)*

EEB
What is it boyo, have you found
something interesting?

TAC
I should say so. Look at these
symbols and pictures, what do you
make of it?

*(Eeb moves closer to the wall
and studies the images and
symbols.)*

EEB
Looks like two men arguing over a
loaf of bread. Seems that the man on
the left is returning the bread to
the vender and the vender doesn't
want it back. What do you make of
it?

TAC
Well, although yours is a colourful
explanation of the events depicted in
the hieroglyphs, I suspect their
meaning is much more complex...

*(Tac points to an object one
of the figures is holding.)*

...See this here, this medallion
shaped object, it looks like he is
trying to give it to this fellow
here, but the fellow doesn't want
it...

    *(Tac moves his hand along the
    scene on the wall.)*

...Now, see here. The man has taken
the object...

    *(Tac moves further along the
    wall.)*

...And now, look here, the man is
trying to give it back.

              EEB
That is what I said, two men fighting
over a loaf of bread.

              TAC
Look at the man on the left, the one
taking the loaf, I mean object. What
strikes you as being peculiar about
his appearance?

              EEB
He is wearing a red turban on his
head in the first picture and in the
last picture he is also wearing a red
turban.

                    TAC
What's odd about that?

                    EEB
Everyone knows when you go to return
something to a vender you leave your
turban at home. The first thing he
will do in a fight is knock it off
your head.

                    TAC
I didn't know that...

          (Tac looks closer at the
          images.)

...Look at the images Eeb, when the
man takes the bread - I mean object,
he is old, when he tries to give it
back he is young.

                    EEB
Maybe we should be reading it from
right to left?

                    TAC
I never thought of that. No, you
have to read it this way because in
the first image he has no bread...

          (Tac throws his hands in the
          air.)

...Blast it Eeb, object!

                    EEB
Well, what does it mean?

                    TAC
If I am reading these hieroglyphs
correctly, the man on the left was
offered eternal life. He initially
took it and was very happy, then at
some point, he didn't want it any
more.

                    EEB
That's gratitude for you. No wonder
that other chap was so upset.

     *(Below them, further down the
     hole, Eeb and Tac hear
     voices.)*

                    TAC
Listen, what's that?

                    EEB
That must be Nelson and MacTavish.

                    TAC
I'd forgotten about them. Better go
and see what they're up to.

Scene fades.

ACT 3. SCENE 3

2.15pm, Friday 17th October, 2025. At aunt Hazzie's farmhouse, Yuri and Dmitry have been waiting for an opportunity to avoid the multitude of people milling around the grounds searching for Spanish coins. The track leading to the main road is thinning out and looks clear enough to travel on. After a moment of contemplation, they decide to seize the opportunity and leave. Downstairs, groups of hungry scavengers are making their way into the kitchen. Hazzie tells a woman with a truckle of blue cheese and goats to take a seat.

                    HAZZIE
Would you like some soup?...

          (*Hazzie looks at all the
          children dressed as cheese
          and goats and smiles.*)

...It's lovely and fresh, made it just this morning.

                    WOMAN
Speak up children. What do you say?

               CHOIR OF CHILDREN
Yes, please.

(Hazzie starts to ladle some soup into several bowls and passes it around the table. Yuri and Dmitry descend the stairs and see Hazzie dishing it out.)

YURI

I must say, I feel for those children.

(Dmitry whispers to Yuri.)

DMITRY

Let's slip out the back and go through woods.

(Yuri and Dmitry put on their masks and enter some woods at the back of the house. They circumvent the crowds of people and head back to the track.)

YURI

The nettles were a bit fierce back there. I got one caught on my forearm, right on that scrape I got earlier. I tell you Dmitry, I was ready to sock that Moon Man in the mouth.

DMITRY

What Moon Man?

YURI

Oh, I forgot to tell you. When I
came out of the newsagent, a man
dressed as a crescent moon
deliberately tripped me up. I fell
and hurt my arm. That's when I saw
the police and we left town.

(Dmitry and Yuri come out of
the woods and stand on the
track.)

DMITRY

I don't think you'll see him again,
you will have to vent your aggression
on someone else.

(Up the track, Dmitry and
Yuri see a police wagon
coming towards them.)

YURI

What shall we do?

DMITRY

Just act nonchalantly and carry on
down track. It will look like we are
walking home...

(Dmitry and Yuri walk towards
the police wagon and it

drives past them.)

...Looks like we are in the clear.

> *(The police wagon hits the brakes and a policeman gets out.)*

POLICEMAN
You two! Stop there...

> *(Dmitry and Yuri keep walking. The policeman pulls out his gun.)*

...You two, the frog and the bear, stop walking or I will shoot. Turn and face me...

> *(Yuri and Dmitry stop walking and turn to face the policeman.)*

...Keep your hands where I can see them...

> *(The policeman shouts to the sergeant.)*

...Sergeant Golovsky, bring the gun. We have them now.

YURI
Dmitry, look in the back of that police wagon, it's that crescent Moon

Man I was talking about.

DMITRY
It's a pity the moon is not out, we could have made a run for it.

(The policeman walks closer
to Dmitry and Yuri.)

POLICEMAN
Now, take off your masks so I can see your faces...

(Dmitry and Yuri take off
their masks.)

...That's them sergeant, shoot them.

(Before Dmitry and Yuri can
move they are shot in the
chest and they fall to the
ground.)

YURI
Dmitry, I... I...

Scene fades.

ACT 3, SCENE 4

4.32pm, Friday 17th October, 2025, Numenobman lake, Russia. George London and his gang of ex-SAS soldiers are being held captive at the Russian encampment in two steel cages. Each cage is approximately 10ft x 8ft and loosely chained to the ground. Each cage holds three red-faced occupants that look on at a bustling, productive encampment. Frogmen continually rise to the surface and hand over cogs, wheels, springs and brass mechanisms to bright-eyed boatmen. When their boats are full, they return to the shore and unload the plunder to an excited group of men in white coats. Soldiers patrol the area and look ready for any eventuality. Outside the cage, a sentry watches over London and his band of misfits with an AK-47 assault rifle. Cavendish scornfully looks at the guard then paces his cage to keep warm.

CAVENDISH
This is your fault London. You're an idiot.

*(Cavendish is in the other
cage to London, some 3 feet
away. London shares his cage
with Pilkington and Lt.*

Commander Cartwright.)

LONDON
Don't you think you would be better
off coming up with a plan to get us
out of here than wasting your time
calling me names?

CAVENDISH
No, you're an idiot, you and that
stupid Pilkington you've got in there
with you. Lighting a fire. I ask
yeh. Don't know where the pair of
you got your training, must have been
at Butlins. My five year old son's
got more brains than you two put
together.

LONDON
Yes, well alright Cavendish, you've
made your point. Stop going on about
it like a nagging wife. It's not at
all constructive, and poor old
Pilky's gone red in the face with
embarrassment.

CARTWRIGHT
He's not embarrassed, he's escaping
old fellow.

        *(Cartwright is a thin man in
        his 60's with a monocle. He
        walks towards London.)*

                    LONDON
Escaping, what do you mean?

                  CARTWRIGHT
He's got one of those balloon jack
thingies. You just dig a small hole,
push it underneath and start blowing.

(London looks on amazed.)

                    LONDON
How much can it lift?

                  CARTWRIGHT
Pilky old boy, London wants to know
how much it can lift?...

         (Pilkington points at his
         face to indicate he can't
         stop blowing. At this point,
         Pilkington's face is bright
         red.)

...He can't speak just now, but I've
seen a car lifted up about 2 feet.

                    LONDON
Two feet. That's more than enough to
get under...

         (London looks at the bottom
         of the cage, it is starting
         to rise.)

...That's it Pilky, good show...

  (London turns and faces
  Cavendish.)

...Well, what do you think of old
Pilky now?

      CAVENDISH
Looks just like a normal balloon to
me. That'll never work...

  (Pilkington blows one last
  puff and the balloon bursts
  with a loud bang. The cage
  falls back to the ground and
  Pilkington collapses in a
  heap in the corner of the
  cage. The Russian sentry
  rushes over to investigate.)

...Like I said, you haven't got the
brains you were born with.

      LONDON
Y'know Cavendish, you're not just a
stinker, you're a bounder. If I get
out of this cage, I'm going to give
you a good thrashing.

     RUSSIAN SENTRY
What is happening?

  (London points towards

Pilkington.)

                    LONDON
One of my officer's is having a heart
attack, we need a doctor.

        *(The Russian sentry moves
        closer to the bars and London
        grabs his head and bashes it
        against the cage. The sentry
        faints.)*

                    LONDON
Cartwright, take this chaps keys from
his belt, I can't hold him much
longer...

        *(Cartwright grabs the keys
        from the Russian's belt, then
        London lets go.)*

...Quickly, undo the lock and let the
others out...

        *(Outside of the cages the
        group huddle together on
        their knees.)*

...Cavendish, I am prepared to forgo
our fisticuffs until after our
escape, if that's alright with you?

                    CAVENDISH
That's the first logical thing you've

said. I'd like to get out of here.

                    LONDON
Yes, well, I think we ought to
salvage something from this mission
before we leave, especially now we
are at the exact location we want to
be...

     (London looks around.)

...Cavendish, this is what I want you
to do. Take Carter and Winslow to
that big tent over there, the one
they've been putting all the stuff
from the lake in. Grab what you can
and we will rendezvous at the other
side of those trees...

     (London points at some trees
     towards the north.)

...I'll take Pilky and Cartwright
over to the radio room and contact
headquarters...

     (London stands up.)

...And remember, destroy as much as
you can and keep your head low...

     (London rummages through the
     pockets of the unconscious
     sentry. He takes a lighter,
     a knife and two grenades.)

...Cavendish, you take the rifle and one grenade. Carter you take the knife and I'll take the hand gun. Pilky, you have the lighter and Cartwright, you take the other grenade...

> *(London hands Cavendish the grenade and the rifle with some extra magazines. He puts the hand gun behind his trouser belt and hands Carter the knife, Pilky the lighter and Cartwright the other grenade.)*

...Right, let's get going. Good luck chaps. See you on the other side.

                    WINSLOW
I haven't got anything?

> *(Winslow is a small wiry fellow in his 70's with bad eyesight. He is an expert with explosives and electronic equipment.)*

                    LONDON
What's that Winslow?

                    WINSLOW
I haven't got anything?

                    LONDON
Well, what can I say...

          (*London puts his hand in his
          pocket and pulls out a
          sweet.*)

...Sometimes life isn't fair.

          (*London looks at the sweet.*)

...Look, here's something for you.

          (*London hands him the sweet.*)

                    WINSLOW
A Humbug?

                    LONDON
That's not just any old Humbug, that
comes from Mellets & Sons on oxford
street. A fine establishment founded
in the 1840's, renowned for their
high quality sugar confections...

          (*Winslow looks at the sweet.*)

...Make it last Winslow, savour every
moment.

          (*London looks at the men one
          last time.*)

                    LONDON
Well, if there isn't anything else, I
suggest we get going.

          *(The two teams split up and
          run towards their appointed
          destinations.)*

Scene fades.

ACT 3, SCENE 5

On planet EgÁs, Tac and Eeb climb down the steps to meet up with Nelson and MacTavish. In front of them is a huge metal door 20ft high and 10ft wide. On the walls there are more hieroglyphs and large sections of symbols belonging to the ancient EgÁsian Language of Es-RevÉr. Nelson and MacTavish are pressing buttons by the door and thumping the panel.

                    MACTAVISH
Auch, stupid thing must be stuck.

                      TAC
Ah, Nelson, MacTavish. What have you two been up to?

                    MACTAVISH
We have bin tryin' tae open yon door, but it's stuck solid...

        (MacTavish is an orange-faced
        EgÁsian with dark brown
        freckles who likes alcoholic
        beverages and is often seen
        drunk. His dialect is
        difficult to understand and
        requires a keen ear. He
        nudges Nelson's elbow.)

... Isnae that richt Nelson?

NELSON
Yes, pressed all those buttons we
did, but nothing happened. Just gave
me a sore finger.

        *(Nelson holds up his index
        finger.)*

                TAC
Yes, well...

        *(Tac puts on his glasses and
        starts to read the symbols on
        the wall.)*

...I'll see if I can read some of
these symbols, it might tell us how
to get in...

        *(Tac moves slowly along the
        wall and reads aloud.)*

...WenÁ NiÁga Evil l-liw walC sbe-aR
fo s-re-taw eulb eh-t sk-nird D.N.A
kazanÁkra fo noill-Ádem dercas eh-t
sd-loh ohw eh...

        *(Tac reads it again to
        himself. The others look
        on.)*

...Yes, well, I think I have it.
Roughly translated it says, *'HE WHO
HOLDS THE SACRED MEDALLION OF
ARKANAZAK AND DRINKS THE BLUE WATERS*

*OF RA-EB'S CLAW WILL LIVE AGAIN
ANEW'.*

                    EEB
I think you must have been right boyo
about that bread hieroglyph. It
being a medallion and not a Cob loaf
like I thought.

                    TAC
It would appear so Eeb.

                    MACTAVISH
Fit I'm needin' tae ken is, does it
tell us how tae open this door.

                    TAC
No, it doesn't, but it does tell us
that our ancestors had discovered the
secret of immortality...

        *(Tac looks at the bottom of
        the door.)*

...Have you tried that big metal
button on the floor?

        *(Tac points at a big round
        metal button on the floor in
        front of the door.)*

                    MACTAVISH
Weel, I hadn't clocked that laddie.
I will give it a try...

(MacTavish presses the button with his foot and the door begins to open. As it opens, huge overhead lighting starts to come on one by one to illuminate the area inside.)

...Holy moly, are yoo seeing this?

(Inside the vault, they see a huge chamber filled with computers, reel to reel tapes, large mechanical machinery, cogs, metal wheels, glass screens, big toothed gears, hanging green crystals and far off into the distance - The Great Council of Arkanazak on their thrones looking over the chamber.)

TAC
We better go and get Sir Daot before we go in.

MACTAVISH
Auch, dinna bother the ol' fool, he'll be ha'in' his afternoon nap. Let's just go and hae a quick look.

TAC
Yes, well, he did mention his sciatica was playing him up. I

suppose it'll be alright...

> *(Tac hands Eeb his torch and
> Eeb lays it down on the steps
> with his own. Tac takes off
> his glasses and starts to
> walk into the chamber.)*

...But MacTavish, I would prefer it
if you didn't refer to Sir Daot as an
old fool.

MACTAVISH
Aye, fit ever you say.

> *(As they walk inside, they
> see layers of dust covering
> everything. On the floor,
> lay the remains of various
> technicians and computer
> operators, just bits of bones
> and white cloth remain.)*

EEB
Boyo? There are a lot of dead bodies
in here. I wonder what happened?

TAC
Just imagine, this vault has been
sealed for over 5,000 years, who
knows what we'll find...

> *(Tac looks at a dead computer
> screen.)*

...I wonder what this thing was,
strange looking contraption.

                NELSON
We must be at least 200ft below the
surface, I wonder what's giving us
all this light?

                TAC
I couldn't say Nelson, but one
thing's for sure, it'll be worth a
fortune. Still working after 5,000
years must be something incredible.

                MACTAVISH
Aye, now yeh talkin'. I could be
spending all my days doon the pub
instead o' walking the desert we you
lot.

                TAC
I wouldn't get your hopes up too high
MacTavish, it's going to take years
to catalogue all this stuff. I mean,
where does one even begin. Don't
even know what to call anything...

        (Tac looks at a broken reel
         to reel machine.)

...Look at this. What am I suppose
to write down for this - Large
rectangle with two wheels and a bit

of tape. I mean, what did it do?
What was its purpose? It would be
the same as a man trying to
understand the intricate workings of
a woman's mind - unfathomable...

> *(Tac brushes some dust away.)*

...And then of course there are the
religious ramifications.

                    EEB
What do you mean boyo?

                    TAC
Well, if we start saying we've
uncovered the vault of The Great
Council of Arkanazak and that they
were a more advanced civilisation
then the one we have now, it's going
to undermine the whole religious
belief system...

> *(Tac turns to face the*
> *group.)*

...Most religious doctrines state
that EgÁs is only 3,000 years old and
that it was created by one of those
alphabet chaps. The very existence
of this chamber now proves that
doctrine to be false. When the news
gets out about what we have
discovered here, there will be total
mayhem.

*(Tac takes a small tin from
his pocket, extracts a red
pill from it and swallows
it.)*

...It's alright saying you believe in
something different to the masses;
you're just dismissed as a fruitcake,
a mooncalf. These expeditions into
the desert to find the Great Council
of Arkanazak and the tomb of King
KÁnTdiE were seen as a lark to them.
Every time we came home empty handed,
it only strengthened their argument,
but finding it, well, that's
something else...

*(Tac moves closer to the
group.)*

...This is the kind of information
that could get us all killed, so when
we get back up top, not a word to
anyone. We shall have to handle this
situation very gingerly...

(Tac turns to Nelson.)

...Nelson, go and wake Sir Daot and
tell him we've found the chamber and
bring him back here. Don't tell
anyone else.

Scene fades.

ACT 3. SCENE 6

5.02pm. Friday 17th October 2025, The Penachy District Jail House. Inside, Kantcoughsky is being moved from a holding cell and escorted to an interview room by two police officers. In the room, he is placed at a table and handcuffed to it. The police officers leave and he is left by himself. Through a double sided mirror, police Sergeant Valery Egorov looks on at Kantcoughsky and talks to a Constable Lebedev.

SGT. VALERY EGOROV
Where can they be? I don't like it when the K.G.B get involved in our cases, they keep you waiting around forever, and when they do finally arrive, they eat all the donuts...

(Sergeant Egorov flicks some ash on the floor from a cigarette.)

...When they get here, don't offer them any coffee, that way, they will not want a donut. Look at that kantcoughsky, he seems troubled.

(Sgt. Valery Egorov is a 43 year old fat man with a horseshoe moustache. His

*pale blue suit no longer fits
him and his shoes are worn
down at the heel. At his
armpits he sweats profusely.
He is smoking a cigarette and
drinking a coffee from a
polystyrene cup.)*

                CONSTABLE LEBEDEV
What do the K.G.B want with
Kantcoughsky?

                SGT. VALERY EGOROV
He is being accused of bombing a
hotel and the death of 39 people; it
is a terrorist act. All terrorist
acts are investigated by the K.G.B,
it is now standard policy.

                CONSTABLE LEBEDEV
Do you think he did it?

                SGT. VALERY EGOROV
What I think is immaterial, but for
my money, he is involved in some way.

    *(The door in the hallway
    opens and two K.G.B agents
    walk in.)*

                SGT. VALERY EGOROV
Hello, I am Sergeant Egorov.

    (Sgt. Egorov holds out his

hand.)

                    AGENT ORLOV
This is special agent Stepanov, and
I'm agent Orlov...

        *(Orlov and Stepanov shake the
        sergeant's hand.)*

...Has anyone spoken to the suspect
yet?

                    SGT. VALERY EGOROV
No, we were waiting for you.

                    AGENT ORLOV
Good. Shall we...

        *(Agent Orlov holds out his
        hand and motions to Sgt.
        Egorov to lead the way.)*

                    SGT. VALERY EGOROV
Yes, this way.

        *(The door opens and Sergeant
        Egorov, agents Orlov and
        Stepanov walk into the
        interview room where
        Kantcoughsky is. The agents
        take a seat opposite
        Kantcoughsky and the sergeant
        stands by the door. Orlov
        takes out a brown folder and*

lays it on the table.)

                    AGENT ORLOV
Prime Minister Kantcoughsky, I am
agent Orlov and this is my partner,
agent Stepanov...

        *(Agent Orlov opens a
        briefcase and takes out a
        folder.)*

...I see in my notes you have been
read your rights and that you have
asked for your lawyer...

        *(Agent Orlov closes the
        folder.)*

...Yes, mmm. Unfortunately, your
lawyer was involved in an automobile
accident on the way to the jail and
he has been taken to hospital...

        *(Sergeant Egorov throws his
        coffee cup in the bin and
        then stands behind
        Kantcoughsky.)*

                P.M. KANTCOUGHSKY
Was he badly hurt?

                    AGENT ORLOV
A broken leg and some minor bruises.
He'll be out of hospital in a couple

of days.

                    P.M. KANTCOUGHSKY
Then I'll wait. I don't wish to
speak to anyone without my lawyer
present, especially the K.G.B.

                    AGENT STEPANOV
I don't think your lawyer wishes to
see you anymore. We saw him only
this morning, just after the
accident. I believe, as they were
taking him away on a stretcher, he
said something to my colleague to
communicate that point. Could you
refresh my memory agent Orlov?

          *(Agent Orlov takes out his
          note pad and flicks through a
          few pages.)*

                    AGENT ORLOV
Ah, here it is. I'll just choose
some of the highlights. 'No, don't
hurt me anymore, I didn't do
anything.'...

          *(Agent Orlov continues to
          flick through his pad.)*

...Sorry, that's the wrong bit...

          *(Agent Orlov flick through
          his pad again.)*

...Yes, here we are. ...'I won't represent Kantcoughsky anymore, he's a lying, cheating, blackmailer. I only had him as a client because he threatened to expose the truth about my wife. That's how he gets people to do things for him. ...He has a key to a safety deposit box, keeps it around his neck on a gold chain. All his dirty little secrets are in that box. If you can get that key, you'll know everything. ...I won't see him again, I promise.'...

(Agent Orlov turns over the page.)

...And then it was just some irrelevant mutterings, 'Please, please don't hurt my family...'. At that point he fainted.

P.M. KANTCOUGHSKY
What a rat. You can't even trust your lawyer these days...

(Kantcoughsky goes to cough, but can't.)

...I have another lawyer, Felix Botkin. He mainly does contractual stuff, but when needs must. I wish to see him.

AGENT ORLOV
Fine, we will send for him. Sgt.
Egorov, could you see to that?

SGT. VALERY EGOROV
Yes, I will do it now.

*(The sergeant starts to leave
the room.)*

Oh, and Sergeant?...

*(The sergeant Stops in his
tracks.)*

...could you possibly get us some
coffee and donuts. Enough for all
three of us.

SGT. VALERY EGOROV
Yes, of course.

*(Sgt. Egorov leaves the
room.)*

P.M. KANTCOUGHSKY
If you think a cup of coffee and a
donut will make me talk, you will be
disappointed. I won't say anything
until Felix gets here. Now, take me
back to my cell.

AGENT ORLOV
Seems a shame to waste a fine coffee.

I understand they have a machine here
that does bean to cup.

                    AGENT STEPANOV
And the donuts are freshly fried and
sent from the bakers direct. They
had a delivery just as we got here.

                    AGENT ORLOV
That's right, saw the baker's van
pull away as we parked up. What harm
can it do to answer a few simple
questions while we wait for your
lawyer?

                    P.M. KANTCOUGHSKY
The K.G.B never ask simple questions.

                    AGENT ORLOV
Well, how about you tell us your name
and address for the record?

         (Agent Stepanov turns on a
         camcorder which is set up on
         a tripod. It is directed
         straight at Kantcoughsky.)

                    P.M. KANTCOUGHSKY
No, I told you, I want my lawyer.

                    AGENT ORLOV
It is just an address, we already
know where you live, so what is so

bad about telling us information we
already know?

>	*(Kantcoughsky looks straight
>	at agent Orlov.)*

>	P.M. KANTCOUGHSKY
Gorki-221b in Odintsovsky
District, Moscow Oblast. Now, that
is all I am going to say.

>	AGENT ORLOV
That is alright, while we are waiting
on your lawyer, we will go and speak
to Olga, perhaps her tongue is a
little looser than yours.

>	*(Agents Orlov and Stepanov
>	get up to leave.)*

>	P.M. KANTCOUGHSKY
Wait. Leave Olga out of this, she
docsn't know anything.

>	*(Agent Orlov and Stepanov sit
>	back down.)*

>	AGENT ORLOV
I would say she knows plenty, the
pair of you have been busy little
bees.

>	P.M. KANTCOUGHSKY
What do you mean?

AGENT ORLOV

For the last nine months, the K.G.B
has had 15 agents watching your every
move. We know every Wednesday at 2pm
you met with Olga at the Metrasky
hotel. You always stay in room 101
and pay the staff handsomely for
their discretion. Approximately
three hours later, you are picked up
by your limo and Olga leaves by
taxi...

*(Agent Orlov opens his
folder.)*

...But we are not interested in your
love life, it's what else you do that
concerns us...

*(Agent Orlov picks up a photo
and shows it to Kantcoughsky.
The photo shows a frontal
body shot of a man walking
away from a car carrying a
black bag, another man
getting into a car and the
arm of a woman sitting in the
passenger seat.)*

...We want to know what your
involvement is with this man?

*(Kantcoughsky looks at the
picture.)*

                    P.M. KANTCOUGHSKY
I have never seen him before, who is
he?

                    AGENT STEPANOV
His name is Vadim Schekov.

                    P.M. KANTCOUGHSKY
Why do you think I know him?

                    AGENT STEPANOV
Because the other man in the photo
getting into this car is you, and the
woman is Olga.

                    P.M. KANTCOUGHSKY
Me? That could be anyone, and that
could be anyone's arm. The picture
is not even clear, the background is
out of focus and fuzzy.

                    AGENT STEPANOV
That is true, but after checking the
registration of the vehicle, which
you can see clearly, we came up with
your name. You do own a red 1977
Ford Capri with the registration
number T123 X8U?

                    P.M. KANTCOUGHSKY
Yes, but I may have loaned it to a
friend that day.

*(Agent Orlov picks up four
more pictures and shows them
to Kantcoughsky. He picks
them up one by one.)*

AGENT ORLOV
What about these pictures? Here you
are coming out of the R.K.A Mission
Control Centre at Korolyov with Vadim
Schekov and Vladimir Ushankov, the
head of Spaceflight communications...

*(Agent Orlov picks up another
picture.)*

...And in this one, you met with a
man at the Gorky Park fun fair. He
gave you a black bag and then you
parted company...

*(Agent Orlov picks up another
photo.)*

...In this one, you are at the Museum
of Modern Art talking to General
Nikolai Gerasimov and Vadim
Schekov...

*(Agent Orlov picks up the
last photo.)*

...This picture is my favourite.
This is your house in the country.
In this picture, you are in your
living room drinking with Vadim

Schekov, Vladimir Ushankov, General
Gerasimov, Olga Usakov and the man
from Gorky Park fun fair, who we now
know to be Alexander Khrushchev. Do
you still maintain that you do not
know Vadim Schekov?

        *(Kantcoughsky looks at the
        pictures, smiles, then looks
        up at agent Orlov.)*

            P.M. KANTCOUGHSKY
I take it you have more Photos?

            AGENT ORLOV
Lots more. Over the last 9 months,
we have taken many pictures of you
and your acquaintances, shot video,
bugged your office and your houses
and traced all your phone calls. We
know where you have been, who you
have spoken to and what you've said.

            P.M. KANTCOUGHSKY
Seems like you have been very busy
bees yourself, but I have done
nothing wrong.

            AGENT STEPANOV
Nothing wrong? Perhaps I can break
it down for you. On August 4th this
year, General Gerasimov met with
Alexander Khrushchev at the
Venchsnech 103rd army base. Two

hours later, Khrushchev appears carrying a black bag. Later that day, he hands the bag to you at the Gorky Park Fun Fair. On August 6th, General Gerasimov receives a report from the ammunition depot on the base that several pounds of C4 explosives are missing from the store room. Gerasimov orders a search of the army base, but a report is never officially made and the matter is closed shortly afterwards. On August 7th, you are seen with Vadim Schekov in this photo...

(Agent Stepanov points at the photo of Vadim Schekov walking away from a red Capri.)

...If you look at Schekov's right hand, you will see he is carrying a black bag. On August 29th, Vadim Schekov starts work at R.K.A mission control as an aerospace support engineer. Shortly afterwards, Vadim is seen carrying that same black bag into the Mission Control building. From CCTV cameras within the building, we learn that Vadim stores the black bag in his locker. 14 days later, Vadim is requested to lead a maintenance team up to the International Space Station to repair a computer console they've been having problems with...

> *(Agent Stepanov takes out
> another photo of Vadim
> Schekov talking to Vladimir
> Ushankov outside the shuttle
> on the access service arm.)*

...If you look at this picture, you
can clearly see Vadim Schekov on the
access arm of the launch site talking
with Vladimir Ushankov. In Schekov's
hand you can see that same black
bag...

> *(Agent Stepanov points at the
> black bag in the photograph.)*

...A few weeks later, The
International Space Station is
destroyed. We know you were involved
in its destruction through this black
bag, and this morning, we had
confirmation from the bomb site at
the Four Seasons hotel that C4
explosives were used. Through
forensic investigation, they were
traced back to the 103rd Venchsnech
army base as being part of the
consignment that went missing in
August...

> *(Agent Stepanov sits back in
> his chair.)*

...The evidence against you is
overwhelming. If I was you, I would
come clean and tell us everything.
It's the only way you'll get a
reduced sentence. You're looking at
a very long time in jail Prime
Minister.

> *(Kantcoughsky looks
> momentarily concerned, then
> starts to smile.)*

P.M.KANTCOUGHSKY
You are pulling at straws. So I know
a few people that all carry a black
bag. You can't prove the bag in
these pictures to be the same bag.
Lots of people have a black bag, and
you certainly can't prove it
contained C4 explosives...

> *(Kantcoughsky sits up.)*

...Is this all you have, photographs
of a black bag being held by
different people on different days?

AGENT ORLOV
No, this is just a sample. Between
the video footage and the recorded
conversations we have of you, I would
say you were looking at life in
prison - You conspired to commit
murder and as a result of your
actions over 40 people have died.

P.M. KANTCOUGHSKY
I have done nothing wrong, I only did
what needed to be done. It is true,
my hands are not clean, but you don't
know the full story.

AGENT STEPANOV
Then enlighten us. Tell us who's
behind the bombings and the reason
for them? The real kingpin in all
this is missing and he is never
spoken of. Tell us who he is and
help yourself.

*(Sgt. Egorov walks back in
the room with coffee and
donuts.)*

SGT. VALERY EGOROV
I hope I didn't miss much...

*(Sgt. Egorov hands out the
coffee and donuts.)*

...one for you, another one for you,
and lastly, but no means least, one
for you Prime Minister. I'll put the
donuts in the middle so you can help
yourselves.

P.M. KANTCOUGHSKY
Untie me, I can't eat donuts and
drink coffee with my hands tied.

*(Sgt. Egorov looks at agent
Orlov.)*

                AGENT ORLOV
Untie him, I don't think he will be
any trouble.

        *(Sgt. Egorov unties
        Kantcoughsky.)*

            P.M. KANTCOUGHSKY
That is better...

        *(Kantcoughsky drinks some
        coffee.)*

...Plaaagh! That is not bean to cup,
that is cheap nasty instant coffee...

        *(Kantcoughsky picks up a
        donut and takes a bite.)*

...Stale! Nothing worse than a stale
donut.

        (He looks at the donut.)

...And look, somebody has licked the
frosting off and left a thumb print
on the side.

        *(He throws it back in the box
        and looks at agent Orlov and
        Stepanov.)*

...You two clowns should work in an advertising agency, I was really looking forward to some refreshments - It is like everything in life, the idea is better than the reality. I don't wish to speak anymore get me my lawyer!

                    AGENT ORLOV
Okay, I think we are done here for the time being...

        (Agent Orlov looks up at Sgt. Egorov.)

...Sgt. Egorov, did you remove a gold chain with a key on the end of it from Prime Minister Kantcoughsky?

                SGT. VALERY EGOROV
Yes.

                    AGENT ORLOV
Could you get the custody officer in charge to bring it to your office, I wish to see it?

Yes, I'll do it right now.

                P.M. KANTCOUGHSKY
I don't know what you want with that key, the lady at the *Lucky Spin Laundrette* gave it to me so I could wash my clothes for free.

AGENT ORLOV
Then you won't mind me looking at it.
Put him back in his cell.

*(Agents Orlov and Stepanov
leave the room.)*

P.M. KANTCOUGHSKY
Sergeant, what time is dinner?

*(Sgt. Egorov looks at his
watch.)*

SGT. VALERY EGOROV
It's at 5pm sharp, so you've missed
it. It's 5.19pm now.

*(They walk out of the room
and into the corridor.)*

P.M. KANTCOUGHSKY
If I gave you some money would you go
and get me a pizza?

SGT. VALERY EGOROV
Sorry, no outside food is permitted
at the jail without authorisation
from the warden.

P.M. KANTCOUGHSKY
But I am your Prime Minister?

                    SGT. VALERY EGOROV
Sorry. Rules are rules. There's a
vending machine at the end of the
corridor, I'll get you a packet of
crisps.

Scene fades.

ACT 3, SCENE 7

5.21pm. Friday 17th October 2025, Numenobman lake, Russia. The last rays of sunshine are falling on the lake and the Russian soldiers are waiting for mess call. London, Pilkington and Cartwright sit behind large boxes of ammo and equipment. For the last ten minutes, activity surrounding the communications tent has been lively with various Russian soldiers entering and exiting with orders. Finally, a lull in activity gives them an opportunity to enter the tent unnoticed.

LONDON
Pilky, I think we can make a move now. You take the left flank and keep a lookout for unwanted visitors and Cartwright...

(London looks at Cartwright.)

...and Cartwright, you take the right. I'll go down the middle.

(London, Pilkington and Cartwright move into the tent. At a table, two Russian soldiers sit by a communications radio looking at a magazine, laughing at

*the pictures and pointing at
various sections. The radio
is playing music - a Russian
Polka. London walks slowly
towards them with his gun in
his hand. Pilkington keeps
watch outside and Cartwright
picks up a bread knife he has
just found on a table next to
a loaf. London creeps closer
to the men who are engrossed
in their magazine and coshes
them on the head with the
butt of his gun. They fall
to the floor unconscious.)*

LONDON
There, that should hold them for a
little while...

*(Cartwright joins London at
the radio and Pilkington
continues to keep a look
out.)*

...Now, let's see if we can get a
hold of old Windbag at H.Q.

*(London takes a seat and
moves the dial on the radio
to BROADCOM 7.9GHS, flips a
switch reading TRANSMIT and
twists a knob past LUXEMBURG,
COPENHAGEN, ZURICH AND
HELSINKI and stops on*

ENGLAND.)

...This is Red Squirrel calling Tiny
Tim. Over.

(The radio transmits static.)

...This is Red Squirrel calling Tiny
Tim. Over.

(A voice is heard.)

                LUCAS B. WINDBAG
This is Tiny Tim. Report. Over.

                LONDON
Mission compromised, need immediate
extraction. Over.

                LUCAS B. WINDBAG
Do you have the package? Over.

                LONDON
Still working on package, hope to
obtain parcel in next ten minutes.
Need extraction for 21.00 hours at
designated pick-up point. Possible
hostile fire and hot L.Z. Request
air cover. Over.

                LUCAS B. WINDBAG
Cherry Picker now en route,
extraction set for 21.00 hours.
Over.

LONDON
Good Show. Over.

LUCAS B. WINDBAG
Good luck Red Squirrel. Over.

LONDON
Many thanks Tiny Tim. Over and Out.

*(London puts down the radio
microphone and gets to his
feet.)*

PILKINGTON
Hurry up, someone is coming?

*(Pilkington hides inside the
tent and a Russian soldier
walks in. Cartwright throws
his knife and the Russian
soldier falls to the floor
clutching his face.)*

LONDON
I say, nice shot old boy. Straight
between the eyes with the butt of the
knife. Knocked him straight out...

*(London walks over to the
Russian soldier lying on the
floor, picks up the knife and
hands it back to Cartwright.)*

...I must say, you certainly are a

dab hand with that thing, I seem to
cut all my fingers slicing an onion.

                    CARTWRIGHT
Just practice, that's all, sir. I
broke my pelvis when I was twelve
trying to scale a drain pipe. Spent
the next fourteen weeks in hospital
throwing a carving knife at a 'Drink
More Milk' poster.

                    LONDON
Time well spent, I would say. Now,
to matters at hand. Let's join up
with Cavendish and the others.

          (London, Pilkington and
          Cartwright exit the tent and
          run for cover behind a truck.
          Several guards have stopped
          for a smoke and a chat
          outside of the collection's
          tent and are stopping them
          advancing. Boats are making
          their way back to shore with
          piles of valves and cogs.
          Inside the collection's tent,
          Cavendish, Carter and Winslow
          are rummaging through the
          spoils.)

                    CARTER
I must say, this is a load of old
junk. Someone is 'avin' a laugh. I

mean look at it...

> (Carter holds up a broken
> piece of cog. Carter is 65
> and is a brash, straight
> talking cockney who still
> thinks he's a dandy.)

...If this is the struggles and
efforts of an advanced alien society,
I'll eat my cap...

> (Carter picks up a valve.)

...A valve? I remember these when I
was a boy. My old man was always
telling me to go and get him a
Mullard GZ32 valve from the corner
shop. He was always pokin' about in
the back of a radio. That's what my
dear ol' mum used to say to him, *'You
pokin' about in the back of that
thing again?'*...

> (Carter throws the valve back
> on the table.)

...And then she would tell him that
he didn't know what he was doin' and
that he'd break something...

> (Carter walks down the line
> of alien artefacts.)

...And then he would say, *'I'll break*

you in a minute!'

> *(Carter picks up a piece of signage and throws it back in the pile.)*

...And then he would push too hard on a valve and break it. That's when he would send me round the corner shop for a new one...

> *(Carter picks up a metal rod 3 feet long with some hair on the end and then throws it back in the pile.)*

What a load of ol' dross. This is what my grandfather would 'ave called *'detritus'*. City gent he was, up there with the upper echelons of society. Some say he had a sense of nobility about him like that of a swan; big, tall fella he was with a long neck and a bent nose. Worked down the sewers as a Tosher - died when they opened the sluice gates unexpectedly...

> *(Carter examines some brass knobs.)*

...They found him a couple of days later with his pockets full of stuff he'd collected in the sewer: gold chains, pearls, rings, coins, mantel

clocks, paintings, watches and some
boiled sweets...

> (*Carter throws the knobs back
> on the table.*)

...They say that's why he couldn't
get out in time. Too much weight,
kept pullin' him back when the waters
came gushin' in. Just too heavy to
climb out.

                    CAVENDISH
Carter, keep it down. This isn't a
trip down memory lane. Do your job.
Grab what you can. It's not our
place to decide what's important, so
keep your opinions to yourself.

                    CARTER
Yeh, I know that, but this stuff is a
load of old rubbish, even an
unqualified grunt like me can see
that.

                    CAVENDISH
Okay, so it's not what we thought it
was going to be, but that doesn't
mean we don't do our job. Now,
c'mon, let's get out of here.

                    WINSLOW
I haven't got anything yet?

CAVENDISH
What do you mean, what have you been
doing all this time?

WINSLOW
Well, I'm in agreement with Carter,
it's a load of old junk, and if I've
got to make a run for it with my
pockets full of cogs, gears and
valves that weigh more than me, I'd
like to be sure of its origins before
I clatter off down the road.

CAVENDISH
Just take what you can. Now, c'mon
we're going.

> (Winslow grabs a reel to reel
> tape and a large valve and
> puts them under his tunic.
> He also picks up three green
> crystals and a ball of string
> and puts them in his pocket.
> Cavendish makes his way over
> to the front of the tent and
> sees Russian soldiers smoking
> and chatting. At the rear of
> the tent a knife slices a big
> hole and London, Pilkington
> and Cartwright walk in.)

LONDON
I wouldn't go that way if I was you,
I don't think they're planning to

move from that spot for a while. One
of the Soldiers is telling a story
about a mud wrestling fight between
two Russian women named Natalia.

                    CARTER
I'm glad you're 'ere. What do you
make of that?

        (Carter holds up a broken
        metal gear.)

                    LONDON
Looks like something from an old push
bike. How is it relevant to our
situation?

        (Carter waves the cog in the
        air at London.)

                    CARTER
How's it relevant? I'll tell you how
it's bleedin' relevant. This junk is
the reason we've come to Russia to
risk our lives. Look at it, it's a
load of old rubbish and this big
ponce over here...

        (Carter points at Cavendish.)

...Wants us to stuff it down our
trousers and make a run for it.

CAVENDISH
Watch who you are calling a ponce
Carter.

LONDON
Look, I suggest that everyone calm
down, grab what we can and leave.

CARTER
I'll tell you now, I ain't carrying
this stuff nowhere, and neither is
he...

(Carter points at Winslow.)

...ain't that right Winslow?

WINSLOW
Well, I am in agreement with Carter,
but at the same time, I would like to
leave.

LONDON
Winslow, I never thought of you as a
mutineer. To think, I gave you my
last Humbug.

WINSLOW
And I appreciate it, believe me I do,
it was very tasty. I could almost
see the confectioner stirring the
sugar in the cauldron with his big
wooden spoon.

                    LONDON
I don't think we can afford to argue
about this anymore, I think the boat
has just landed again with another
delivery of artefacts.

                    CARTER
Good. Let's get out of here, but I
ain't carrying this stuff.

        *(Carter throws the cog on the
        table and the table collapses
        making a huge metallic
        sound.)*

                    LONDON
Run for it lads, the games up.

Scene fades.

ACT 4. SCENE 1

6.02pm. Friday 17th October 2025, seven miles past the Oka river bridge, near the town of Kaluga, Russia. In a secret underground bunker, two bodies stir in a dingy, dank concrete cell. They are wearing bright orange overalls and have no shoes on their feet. In the cell, two cast iron beds sit opposite one another and a broken sink and toilet bowl offer the en suite amenities.

YURI
Ooh, what is that smell?

(Yuri gets to his feet.)

DMITRY
I think it's a broken drain...

*(Dmitry moves from the floor
and sits on the bed.)*

...Yuri, you are alive! I'm alive!
What happened?

YURI
We were shot with a tranquiliser
dart. That big soldier leaned out of
police wagon and shot us.

                    DMITRY
Oh, my head. Everything is fuzzy.
Where do you think we are?

          (A voice comes from another
          cell.)

                    VOICE
You are in the Okan military
installation, 1 mile below the
surface.

                    DMITRY
Who said that?

                    VOICE
I did, I'm in the next cell.

          (In the wall near to the
          ceiling on the east side of
          the cell, a metal air vent
          can be seen. Dmitry and Yuri
          stand next to the wall.)

                    DMITRY
What's your name?

                    VOICE
My name is Viktor Popov. I am in
here with my friend Alexander. He is
sleeping just now, they beat him up
pretty good.

                    YURI
The terrorist Viktor Popov?

                 VIKTOR POPOV
What do you mean terrorist?

                    YURI
The Viktor Popov of the O.F.E?

                 VIKTOR POPOV
That's me, but I am no terrorist.
They have my friend and I blamed for
that bombing at the Four Seasons
hotel, but we were busy handing out
leaflets when it blew up. Who are
you?

                    YURI
I am Yuri Chekov and my friend is
Dmitry Usakov.

                 VIKTOR POPOV
The dead cosmonauts. That is in poor
taste my friend.

                    YURI
It's the truth, we didn't die. We
turned off Dome and stole shuttle
from alien spacecraft and made it
home. We were trying to tell the
world truth when we were shot by a
big soldier and woke up here.

                    VIKTOR POPOV
What are you talking about, what Dome
and spacecraft?

          (Dmitry looks at Yuri and
          puts his index finger to his
          mouth. He whispers to Yuri.)

                      DMITRY
Don't say anymore. It might be a
trap. What are the chances that is
Viktor Popov next door? Leave it to
me...

          (Dmitry walks up to the wall
          vent.)

...Excuse my friend, he has a vivid
imagination and likes to tell
stories.

                    VIKTOR POPOV
Then who are you two guys?

          (A voice comes from the vent
          of the west side of the
          cell.)

                     MOON MAN
I'll tell you who they are - common
thugs. Ruined my day they have, not
to mention my outfit. It's because
of these two I'm in here. If I
hadn't told that policeman I'd

spotted them going in the direction
of the Pyritevich farm I could be
eating a nice sous-vide carrot and
parsnip pudding with my mother.

(*Yuri looks at Dmitry.*)

YURI
It is that crescent moon chap who
tripped me up coming out of
newsagent...

(*Yuri rubs his arm, then
walks over to the west wall.*)

...So, it is your fault we are in
here. When I get out of this cell, I
will pop you in face.

MOON MAN
You're just like all the rest,
flexing your muscles to prove your
manhood. I was only trying to get
back to my poor old mum. She'll be
sitting there all by herself waiting
for me to come home and make her some
supper. All alone she is in a cold
house with only her knitted teddy
bears to keep her company. She must
be sick with worry, and all you can
think about is yourself. It makes me
sick. You criminal types are all the
same - me, me, me.

(*Dmitry takes Yuri's arm.*)

                    DMITRY
Don't engage with him anymore, it is
pointless.

                  VIKTOR POPOV
I still don't know who you or your
strange friend are?

                    DMITRY
That's not important. I believe we
are all on the same side. What can
you tell us about this place?

                  VIKTOR POPOV
It is a military installation for
terrorists and dissidents. Where the
government puts all of its political
nonconformists.

                    DMITRY
Yes, but where is it?

                  VIKTOR POPOV
We are seven miles south of the Oka
river bridge, near the town of
Kaluga. Why do you want to know?

                    DMITRY
I would like to know, so we can
escape.

                  VIKTOR POPOV
Escape? Forget about it. No one who

comes here ever leaves again, except
in a box.

                    DMITRY
Then how do you know about this
place?

                 VIKTOR POPOV
I used to work here 30 years ago. I
was a soldier in the Russian army
assigned to this post for 2 years.
It is a secret base, not even the
president knows of it. I was
transferred here when the war against
the Chinese started. I'll tell you
again, escape is impossible.

                    DMITRY
What do they intend to do with us?

                 VIKTOR POPOV
They will interrogate you for a
while, then beat you. Interrogate
you some more, then shoot you. I
would say you have five days at most.
They always get everything they need
within five days.

          (Yuri walks over to Dmitry
          and pulls him to one side.
          He starts to whisper.)

                    YURI
Dmitry, I am tired of all this. Now

we only have five days to live. I
think we better attack whoever comes
through that door and take our
chances in a rumble.

                    DMITRY
Perhaps, but let's get some more
information from our friend in the
next cell. The more we know about
this place the better our chances are
of escape.

                    YURI
You are right, and you know how to
plan things better than me.

                    DMITRY
Good. Now let's see what this Popov
fellow knows...

        (Dmitry and Yuri walk over to
        the east vent.)

...Viktor, I noticed our cell has a
metal door that needs a key, what is
the rest of the complex like?

        (There is silence for a while
        then Viktor speaks.)

                 VIKTOR POPOV
It seems you are determined to speak
about escape...

(Viktor gets off his bed and walks to the vent.)

...First of all, it is not down here you have to worry about. We are in sector K, one of the first built in 1934. Everything down here is old and easily broken or picked. There are 10 more sectors above this one, each one more modern with more security. Even if you get past the motion sensors, surveillance cameras, biometric hand scanners, armed guards and heat detectors, you'll never open the main door leading to the outside. It's 15 inches thick and needs a voice operated password. The password is changed every week and only army personnel assigned to this installation know what it is. It's never written down, only passed on verbally in a padded room to prevent being overheard by prisoners.

DMITRY
It does seem a challenge, but you must have noticed weaknesses in the system while you were here?

VIKTOR POPOV
Yes, but a lot...

(A key entering a cell door can be heard and it reverberates down the

corridor.)

...Quick, someone is coming, just sit
on your beds and stay quiet. Don't
say anything unless they ask.
Compliance is the only way out.

Scene fades.

ACT 4, SCENE 2

On planet EgÁs, Nelson has entered the tent of Sir Gorf Daot and is out of breath.   Sir Daot is fast asleep on an oval shaped hammock made from the lennef tree, a fine dark hardwood from the Setac region of EgÁs known for its extreme toughness and weight.   The rest of the tent is furnished using the same wood: cupboards, shelving, a wardrobe, dresser with mirror, wind up gramophone and a coffee table.   Over him, two servants wave large paper fans to cool the air.

                    NELSON
Sir Daot, come quick?

                  SIR GORF DAOT
What, what's happening?

                    NELSON
Come quick, they've found it.   They found the Council.

                  SIR GORF DAOT
What?   Where?   I thought Tac was going to look at some steps you'd made for the latrine?

                    NELSON
Yes.   No.   We were digging a latrine,

but then we found the entrance to the
Great Council of Arkanazak's vault.
Tac sent me over here to tell you
we've found it and to come and get
you.

>   *(Sir Daot jumps off his bed
>   and runs outside.)*

>   SIR GORF DAOT
Yippee! Listen up everyone?...

>   *(All of the workmen stop what
>   they are doing and come over
>   to Sir Daot.)*

...We've found it, we've found the
Great Council...

>   *(Everyone shouts with joy and
>   turbans are thrown in the
>   air.)*

...Everyone, go and help yourselves
to some food and drink. You've all
done a fantastic job...

>   *(Sir Daot stops a thin young
>   boy as he hobbles past.
>   Nelson looks on at the
>   excitement and tries to get
>   Sir Daot's attention.)*

...You boy?

                    YOUNG BOY
Who me?

                  SIR GORF DAOT
Yes, you. I want you to run into
town and give this message to the
postmaster at the telegraph office...

        (*Sir Daot scribbles down a
        message: 'To Professor Rellim
        Retlaw of the institute of
        Setac, Feal Yab District,
        MomÁdrac. STOP. Tomb of
        King KÁnTdiE and Great
        Council of Arkanazak found at
        Ra-eb's Claw. STOP. Send
        reporters and photographers.
        STOP. Contact Sir Riffak at
        the Poontac Foundation and
        tell him to bring wagons,
        crates, packing material and
        more help. STOP. Inform
        Nomel Kent at The Daily EgÁs.
        STOP. Yours sincerely, Sir
        Gorf Daot.' He hands it to
        the boy.*)

...Right, now here's the message.
Keep it safe at all times. Now, run
along as fast as you can - speed is
of the essence.

                  YOUNG BOY
Run! What with my leg? Can't you
ask someone else to do it? That will

take me a week with this foot...

>*(The young boy lifts up his*
>*left foot to show Sir Daot.*
>*His big toe is swollen and*
>*his leg is in a wooden*
>*splint.)*

...we are a good 8 miles from the
nearest town, I don't think I could
make it that far!

>*(Nelson is tugging at Sir*
>*Daot's arm.)*

SIR GORF DAOT
Nonsense. Get back here by tonight
with Professor Retlaw's reply and
there'll be an extra slice of meat on
your plate at supper. Now, trot
along...

>*(The boy limps off as fast as*
>*he can and disappears over a*
>*sand dune. Nelson is still*
>*tugging at Sir Daot's arm.*
>*Sir Daot turns to face him.)*

...Yes, yes Nelson what is it?
You've nearly taken the skin off my
arm.

NELSON
Mr. Tac also said that you should
keep the discovery secret just now

and not let anyone know we've found
it.

                SIR GORF DAOT
Why the blazes didn't you tell me?

                  NELSON
I was trying to tell you, but you
wouldn't take me on. Just ignored
me, just like I was nothing. You
were so wrapped up in your own
importance and wanting to tell
everyone how great you was, that I
was just an annoyance. Well, now
look what you've done. Going to look
a right fool when Tac finds out about
this. Told the world about it you
have, and you haven't even had a look
yourself. Tac's going to be proper
mad at you boyo.

        (Sir Gorf Daot has gone red
        in the face and fumbles to
        light his pipe.)

                SIR GORF DAOT
Yes, well these things happen, can't
expect to do the right thing all of
the time. Anyway, this is my
expedition and I'll tell who I bally
well want.

                  NELSON
That's it, go on the defensive.

You're only making it worse for
yourself. Best thing to do is just
confess to your mistake and move on
and call it a learning curve. Your
kind are good with that sort of
thing.

> *(Sir Gorf Daot looks at
> Nelson sternly.)*

                 SIR GORF DAOT
What kind would that be?

                   NELSON
Well, y'know, moneyed folk. Doesn't
matter how many mistakes you lot
make, you just put your hand in your
pocket and the problem goes away...

> *(Sir Gorf Daot puffs on his
> pipe with a rubicund face.)*

...Now, I bet you could kill someone
and not even go to jail.

                 SIR GORF DAOT
Let's put it to the test shall we.

> *(Sir Gorf Daot reaches for a
> knife tucked into his
> shorts.)*

                   NELSON
Now there's no need to be like that

boyo, I was only just saying...

> *(Nelson runs off in the*
> *direction of the vault. Sir*
> *Gorf Daot puts his knife back*
> *into his shorts and puffs his*
> *pipe.)*

                SIR GORF DAOT
Annoying chap.

Scene fades.

ACT 4. SCENE 3

6.22pm. Friday 17th October 2025, Numenobman lake, Tulla, Russia. London and his crew of ex-SAS soldiers make a dash for cover into the nearby woods and crouch down by a fallen oak tree. Behind them, Russian soldiers advance on their position and circle the area to try and out flank them. Gun fire and strange sonic booms can be heard amongst the trees and an officer shouting out orders. Moments later, huge rocks from the 13th century trebuchet land near their position and explode on impact.

                    CARTER
They're a bit nifty with that bleedin' trebuchet, that last attack gave my hair a new parting.

          *(London looks around for an
          escape route.)*

                  CAVENDISH
That's nothing compared to what's about to happen.

                    CARTER
What do mean?

                    CAVENDISH
Take a look at the chap over by that
tree...

          (*Carter looks over the log.*)

...Do you see him?

                    CARTER
What, that small guy who's fumbling
about with his rifle?

                    CAVENDISH
Yes, that's him, but that's no rifle.

                    CARTER
What is it then?

                    CAVENDISH
That's an MT-2 Lock-on Smite
Retaliator. It takes about five
minutes to charge, but when it does,
it locks on to any heat signature
within an 8 metre radius that its
fired at. Thousands of tiny
particles rain down from above like
pins of pain. You feel sick for a
few minutes, then you blow up like a
balloon and explode...

          (*Carter is still watching the*
          Russian charge his weapon.)

...It's a mechanical and chemical

based weapon - deadly.

                    CARTER
Well, don't just bloody sit there,
throw your grenade...

        (Cavendish throws his grenade
        and the soldier blows up.)

...Let's get out of here.

        (They all run east towards a
        clearing that heads upwards
        over rocky terrain.)

                    LONDON
Don't give up lads, keep going,
that's the ticket.

                    WINSLOW
It's alright for you, you're not
carrying anything. This valve is
like a balloon in my trousers.

                    LONDON
I thought you weren't carrying
anything Winslow, I thought you'd
shacked up with Carter.

                    WINSLOW
I didn't say I hadn't taken anything,
I just said I wouldn't.

                    LONDON
Yes, well. Good show.

          *(Constant fire whizzes past
          London and his men.
          Cavendish turns around and
          fires a few shots back at the
          Russians.)*

                  CARTWRIGHT
I don't know how much longer I can
run, I'm not used to this. My legs
are like jelly!

                    LONDON
Keep going. If poor old Pilky can do
it, so can you.

          (Pilkington looks exhausted.)

                  PILKINGTON
I've been holding on to Cartwright's
trousers. He's been pulling me along
the last five minutes. I'm too old
for all this running.

                  CARTWRIGHT
You blighter. No wonder I'm out of
breath. I thought my heart was
giving up on me.

          *(From behind them Russian
          soldiers rally closer and a
          ZX-81 pin wheel is let loose.*

*A high pitched sound screams
into the air and the pin
wheel hurtles towards London
and his gang.)*

                    CAVENDISH
It's a Pin Wheel, take cover. Don't
let them touch you.

                     LONDON
What the bally-hoot is a Pin Wheel
Cavendish?

                    CAVENDISH
Screw shaped tracking devices that
burrow into your skin and lodge
themselves into your bones. Almost
impossible to remove.

          *(A whizz and a whir travel
          past the gang and they all
          dive for cover into a pit.)*

                     LONDON
Everyone get down...

          *(The ZX-81 Pin Wheel whizzes
          past them and explodes on
          impact with a tree.*

...C'mon, let's get out of here!

          *(Darkness has finally fallen
          and London and his men hurry*

*up the hillside as fast as
they can. At the top, they
scurry into a small cave to
rest for a moment. The
Russians aren't far behind
and the sound of a Philo
Plasma Liquefier charging can
be heard throughout the
area.)*

                PILKINGTON
Don't know about you lot, but I'm
about beat. Not used to all this
running about stuff. A leisurely
stroll on a Sunday afternoon is about
my speed.

                 LONDON
Chin up Pilky. At least we're at the
top. Just imagine the fix we'd be in
if it was still daylight...

     *(A loud droning noise is now
     added to the thrum of the
     Philo Plasma Liquefier.)*

...I say, what is all that racket the
Russians are making. They certainly
don't mind giving their position
away. Still, I'm jolly glad we out
ran that trebuchet, blasted medieval
contraption, absolute pest of a
thing.

                    CAVENDISH
I think we've got bigger problems
than we had before...

          (Cavendish looks down in the
          valley below and points to
          two Russians mounting the
          Philo Plasma Liquefier to a
          tripod. London walks over to
          see.)

...You see that, that's a Philo
Plasma Liquefier.

                    LONDON
Yes, I see it. What does it do?

                    CAVENDISH
It turns everything into liquid -
Rocks, trees, metal and people. One
zap from that and its good night
forever.

                    LONDON
What's it's range?

                    CAVENDISH
5-800 metres.

                    LONDON
Why have they stopped. We'll be out
of range when we go down the other
side. Doesn't make any sense. Look,
nobody's chasing us anymore. Right,

c'mon chaps we're moving on.
Something's amiss down there.

                    CARTER
What?   I've only just sat down!

                    LONDON
Carter, I wouldn't complain too much
if I was you, it's your fault we are
in this mess.

          (London and his men start
          their way down the other side
          of the hill when they are met
          with a sudden drop.)

                    CAVENDISH
Nobody move. There's a 600ft drop
straight down.

                    CARTER
That's just terrific, what the
bleedin' heck we supposed to do now?

                    CAVENDISH
At least we know why they're not
chasing us anymore.

          (London walks over to the
          edge.)

                    LONDON
We'll never climb down that in the
dark. Blast! If only we hadn't lost
all our equipment...

        (London paces for a moment.)

...They'll probably wait an hour or
two, then move in to out flank us.
We can't go forward and we can't go
back down that's for sure. Back to
the cave lads, let's have a rest for
ten minutes and see if we can
brainstorm our way out of this
situation.

Scene fades.

ACT 4, SCENE 4

7.12pm. Friday 17th October 2025, Okan military installation, Russia. Inside their new home, Dmitry and Yuri are dealing with the situation at hand. Dmitry is in conversation with Viktor Popov extracting vital information and Yuri is fast asleep and is curled up on a cast iron bed covered by a green woollen sheet.

VIKTOR POPOV
...And if you fold the paper again you end up with an African elephant.

DMITRY
I see. It is a pity I don't have any paper...

> *(Dmitry moves his hands to fold a piece of invisible paper.)*

And in only 17 moves. Seems impossible.

VIKTOR POPOV
I could prove it, if I wasn't in this cell...

> *(Victor yawns and sits down on his bed.)*

...Now, if you will excuse me, I am
going to get a nap.

          (Dmitry paces the cell for a
          few minutes and watches Yuri
          sleep. He returns to the
          vent.)

                    DMITRY
Viktor?

                    VIKTOR POPOV
Yes, what is it now?

          (Dmitry puts his mouth up to
          the vent and whispers.)

                    DMITRY
You said earlier that you might be
able to help us with our escape?

                    VIKTOR POPOV
Not that again, I thought we'd moved
past that.

                    DMITRY
I only have a few questions.

          (Viktor moves from his bed
          and goes over to the vent.)

                    VIKTOR POPOV
Alright, but be quick. The guards

are due shortly. What do you want to
know?

                    DMITRY
How do we get out of this cell and
reach the upper levels?

          (*Yuri begins to snore.*)

                    VIKTOR
The best plan is to wait. At some
point they will take you for
questioning. This usually takes
place on level C, so you only have to
get to level A from that point. This
would be your best time to create a
diversion and try to escape. The
difficulty you now face is that in
order to leave level C and B you need
to use a hand scanner to get into the
lift. That means you will need to
take a hostage to operate it or chop
off someone's hand.

                    DMITRY
What about the layout, how big is
each level?

                    VIKTOR
This is the tricky part. Each level
is over a mile in each direction.

                    DMITRY
What! How are we going to find our

way out, it's too big?

                    VIKTOR
As long as you head in one direction
- east, west, north, south, it
doesn't matter. There are only 4
lifts on each section, so choose a
direction and run. I suggest you run
east because the interrogation rooms
are on that side of the building and
you will have a shorter distance to
cover. If you are lucky, you will be
able to grab a cart off of someone
and make a dash to the lift.   The
lifts are located in the middle of
the end walls and are indicated by a
red or orange line. If you see a red
line, go to your right. If you see
an orange line, go to your left.

                    DMITRY
Wait a minute, let me try and
remember this. I don't have anything
to write with...

          (Dmitry goes over to Yuri who
          is still snoring and pushes
          his shoulder.)

...Yuri, wake up?

                    YURI
What is it now?

                    DMITRY
I need a pen and paper.

                    YURI
You have woken me up for a pen. I
was eating a lovely supper of lobster
and sweet corn soup. I had added
bacon lardons that had been gently
glazed with maple syrup. It was
quite tasty. Now I am back here with
scratchy cover.

                    DMITRY
This is important Yuri, you want to
get out of here don't you?

                    YURI
Why? We will only get straight back
into another fix.

                    DMITRY
Do you have a pen and paper or not?

                    YURI
Yes, yes. Just wait. Here...

        (Yuri hands Dmitry a 2B
        pencil.)

...Use this pencil. You are very
lucky they left me my cigarettes. I
always keep a small pencil in my
cigarette carton for emergencies.
You should know cosmonauts have

pencils not pens, pens are not
reliable and you can't cut them in
half. A 2B pencil is the best grade
of pencil you can carry, not too
dark, not too light, much better than
anything in the 'H' Range...

(Dmitry interjects Yuri.)

                    DMITRY
...C'mon Yuri, I don't need a lesson
in the gradation of pencils. Do you
have any paper?

   *(Yuri rips out a piece of
   paper from his cigarette
   packet and hands it to
   Dmitry.)*

                    YURI
Here, now let me be. Wake me up when
they serve dinner.

   *(Dmitry walks back over to
   the wall near the vent
   quickly scribbling down
   notes.)*

                    DMITRY
Okay, I am back.   I have written it
down so far. What happens next?

                    VIKTOR
After you have made it to the lift,

you must scan the hand of a member of
staff. Make sure you have taken a
staff member who carries a green pass
and has access to all areas. If you
don't, and you take somebody who
carries a blue pass, like a janitor,
you will be locked out of every door
and access panel when they activate
the total lockdown procedure. At
this point it is game over. While
you are stuck in the lift pressing
all the buttons like a person
possessed, a poisonous gas will enter
via the roof vent and you will be
dead in 15 seconds along with the
janitor...

*(Viktor moves his position
and walks away from the vent,
then back again.)*

...if however you have grabbed a
person with a green pass, you will
still be able to move freely through
the complex unhindered by the total
lockdown protocol. By now, I am sure
everyone will know what you are doing
and every armed guard the
installation has will be making their
way to the lift you are in.

*(Dmitry scribbles down some
notes at lightning speed.)*

DMITRY
Wait a minute. I need another piece
of paper...

     (Dmitry walks over to Yuri.
     Yuri has fallen back asleep.)

...Yuri, wake up! I need more paper.

     (Yuri Stirs.)

YURI
Dmitry, you are pest. The waiter was
just bringing the main course. A
lovely thick 32oz sirloin steak with
a wonderful big piece of fat on the
edge...

     (Yuri stands up and takes out
     his cigarettes, lights one,
     then hands another piece of
     paper to Dmitry.)

...I will sit here and smoke for a
while until you have finished
plotting our escape.

DMITRY
I am glad you have realised it is for
our benefit and not just mine.

YURI
Yes, I realise it is for both our
benefits, but it will only bring more

death.

                    DMITRY
Sometimes, people have to die so
others can live. If I have to kill
someone, so be it...

     *(Dmitry walks back to the
     vent.)*

...Viktor, I am back.

     (There is no answer.)

...Viktor, are you there?

                    VIKTOR
Yes. Alexander is dead.

                    DMITRY
What?

                    VIKTOR
Alexander is dead. He must have died
from internal bleeding. They really
let him have it.

                    DMITRY
I am sorry to hear about Alexander.
How long did you know him for?

                    VIKTOR
15 years.

DMITRY
That is a long time. Now what
happens?

VIKTOR
What?

DMITRY
What happens next? We are in the
lift and the guards are rushing
towards us. What do we do now?

VIKTOR
I have just told you my good friend
has died and you are continuing to
ask me questions about a pointless
escape. Do you have no sense of
propriety?

MOON MAN
That's just what I said to his friend
when he fell over my foot. They're
both the same, only interested in
their own importance. That Dmitry's
worse than the other one. Imagine
asking you that after your friend's
just died. Don't pay them no mind
Viktor, they're both rotten. It's a
shame you're not in here with me, I
would console you in your hour of
need.

     (Dmitry walks over to the
     west wall.)

                    DMITRY
How long have you been listening to
our conversation?

                   MOON MAN
Since the start. Well, there isn't
any telly in here is there. What did
you want me to do, put my fingers in
my ears?

          *(Yuri stands up and puffs his
          cigarette.)*

                     YURI
You are a worm. What are you going
to do now? I suppose you will tell
the guard we are planning to escape?

                   MOON MAN
Maybe. I haven't decided.

          *(Dmitry walks over to the
          east wall.)*

                    DMITRY
Viktor, I am sorry. But we must get
out...

          *(Outside in the corridor a
          door is being opened.)*

...Viktor? They are coming for us,
please tell me the next step.

(*The noise outside in the
corridor gets louder and
screaming from another cell
can be heard.*)

VIKTOR
Are you really Dmitry Usakov?

DMITRY
Yes. I know it sounds improbable,
maybe even impossible, but it's the
truth. Yuri and I made it back from
the International Space Station and
we need to tell everyone what really
happened up there; the truth about
our planet and the lies the
government have covered up for years.
If you don't help us Viktor, no one
will ever know and the truth will die
with us.

(*There is a silence for a
moment.*)

VIKTOR
I will tell you...

(*Viktor tells Dmitry the last
part of the escape plan and
Dmitry quickly scribbles it
down. Outside the cell, the
sound of gun shots ring out
followed by a clang and a
thud - then silence.*)

...So, as you can see, it's
impossible. If you don't know the
password it is all in vain!

*(The door to Viktor's cell
opens and Dmitry and Yuri
listen from their cell.)*

                    THE GUARD
Viktor? Time's up!

*(Two gun shots are heard,
followed by a body hitting
the floor. The cell door
closes and the guard walks
away.)*

                    YURI
Dmitry, they have killed him.

*(Dmitry puts his bits of
paper in his pocket.)*

                    DMITRY
Yes.

Scene fades.

ACT 4, SCENE 5

Friday 17th October, 7.22pm.   In a cave, on a hillside, overlooking the Numenobman lake, London rallies his men together to talk over their options. Winslow is removing a large valve from his left trouser leg and extracting other objects from his pockets: string, a reel to reel tape and 3 green crystals. Cavendish is also lightening his load by throwing a pile of metal rods and brass cogs on the ground. Cartwright, Pilkington and Carter look on and await for London's plan of action.

LONDON
Gather round chaps...

*(Everyone moves a bit closer
and London pulls out a map
from his tunic.)*

...As you know, we've got ourselves
in a bit of a sticky wicket. Below
us, we have that wretched liquefying
machine and enemy forces moving in
from both the left and right flanks.
Ahead of us is a 600ft drop which is
suicide without some sort of light to
guide the way...

(London unfolds his map.)

*...Pilky, do you still have
your lighter?*

                PILKINGTON
Yes.

                LONDON
Hand it over old bean, need to see
this map...

        *(Pilkington hands over the
        lighter. London flips it and
        it bursts into flame.)*

...That's better. If you look here
chaps...

        *(London points at the map and
        moves his finger along a
        track.)*

...This is where we are, and this is
where we need to be for 9pm. It's a
good few miles, I should say at least
six. If we had no obstructions or
hindrances, it would be an absolute
doddle. A fast march and we'd be
there...

        (The lighter goes out.)

...Blast this thing. What a pity we
lost all our equipment...

        (London flicks the lighter

again.)

...I must say, a decent cup of tea
and a Pikelet would go down a treat
just now...

> *(The lighter goes out once
> more. London flicks the
> lighter again.)*

...Don't even have a torch, what I
wouldn't give for some light.

> *(In the corner of the cave, a
> scratchy sound is heard
> followed by a low hum.)*

CARTER

What's that?

CAVENDISH

Must be a rat or a mountain lion.

WINSLOW

Mountain lion?

CAVENDISH

Aye. Quite big in these parts. Mind
you, it could be a bear. We are in a
cave. They have really big bears in
Russia.

WINSLOW

A bear?

*(London pulls out his
revolver and moves towards
the sound.)*

                    LONDON
Stay still men, I'll handle this.

        *(As London walks towards the
        sound, a bright light beams
        out in every direction.)*

                    CARTWRIGHT
My eyes. I can't see it's too
bright.

        *(The light fades down to
        around 300 watts.)*

                    CARTWRIGHT
It's the valve.

        *(London walks over to
        Winslow's valve. On the
        bottom of the metal
        connectors, 3 green crystals
        have fused themselves tight.)*

                    LONDON
It's Winslow's valve. There appears
to be three green gems or crystals
stuck to the bottom of it. They must
be some sort of power source.

                    CARTER
Bleedin' spooky if you ask me. I
mean how's it working, and how did
those crystals get up and walk over
there and attach themselves to that
valve?

                    LONDON
Haven't got the foggiest notion I'm
afraid Carter. But one thing we do
know that we didn't before.

                    CARTER
What's that?

        (London turns to Carter.)

                    LONDON
It's not all junk.

                    CARTER
I didn't see any crystals, I just saw
rubbish.

                    LONDON
Yes, quite...

        (London walks over to
        Cavendish's pile of metal and
        picks up a 3ft rod.)

...this ought to do the trick...

        (London grabs Winslow's ball

*of string and fastens it to
the end of the metal rod. He
then picks up the valve and
attaches it to the metal rod
using the string.)*

...There. Now we have a torch. I
suggest we get going.

                    CAVENDISH
Where to?

                    LONDON
Down the mountain of course.

                    CAVENDISH
With that thing. It'll probably only
last 10 minutes and we'll be stuck on
the side of a mountain with a 600ft
drop below us, pleading to the
Russians to come and rescue us.
That's just a stupid idea, I say we
stay and fight.

                    LONDON
With what? One hand grenade, a rifle
and a knife. Now that's stupid.
Besides, one does not plead under any
circumstances...

     *(London looks at his new
     creation in awe and smiles.)*

...No Cavendish, this is a sign, a
very positive sign, and I am willing
to bet that this valve will last the
30 minutes to climb down that rock
face. It's lasted 5,000 years in
space, I'm sure it will last another
30 minutes on Earth.

                    WINSLOW
5,000 years?

                    LONDON
Yes Winslow, at least that's what my
report said. Now, I'm going down
this mountain. You can join me or
stay and die, the choice is yours...

          *(London walks off to the
          cliff edge. Everyone follows
          after a few minutes.
          Cavendish is the last to
          come. Winslow walks over to
          London. London shines the
          light down the cliff.)*

...Winslow, look there! Seems to be
a small track.

                    WINSLOW
I'm no goatherd, but I would say
that's a goat trail leading down the
cliff face. It's narrow, but doable.

          (London turns to the group.)

                    LONDON
Listen up chaps. Found a goat path
leading down the mountain. It's a
bit narrow, but if we stay in single
file, I believe it feasible...

        *(A flare shoots up into the
        sky lighting up the area and
        a rustling and movement in
        the trees can be heard.)*

...Looks like they're on to us. Come
on, let's get going.

        *(London and his team of ex-
        SAS soldiers climb down the
        narrow path to a flat plateau
        and take a break. Above
        them, the Russian soldiers
        search for them in the dense
        pine forest and fail to
        discover the goat trail
        leading down the mountain.)*

                    CAVENDISH
Looks like you were right London.

                    LONDON
That can't possibly be Cavendish's
voice, I heard someone say I was
right.

                    CAVENDISH
I still think it's more luck than

skill, but I will admit I was wrong.

LONDON
That's good to hear Cavendish, but
don't think I've forgotten about that
thrashing you're going to get.

CAVENDISH
No, I'm finding it hard to
concentrate worrying about the
thrashing you're gonna give me.

LONDON
I should think so too.

CARTWRIGHT
I think his being sarcastic London.

LONDON
Don't think so Cartwright.

*(Peering over the side of a
high cliff face, London holds
his torch out to see what
lies beneath.)*

CARTER
What can you see?

LONDON
There's a path along this ridge.
Looks a bit tricky, but leads us into
those pine trees over there.

*(London points his finger
into the distance.)*

                CAVENDISH
Then what are we waiting for?

                LONDON
Nothing!

*(They move off and pass
through a small group of pine
trees and come to a clearing
where they hear the sound of
running water.)*

                WINSLOW
Can you hear that?

                CARTWRIGHT
Sounds like water.

*(They run towards the sound
and arrive at a large rock
formation overlooking the
valley below.)*

                LONDON
Stay back! There's a 300ft drop
straight down into a ravine.

                CARTWRIGHT
What do we do now?

*(London shines his torch
along the edge of the rocks
and spies an old rope
bridge.)*

LONDON

Look! A bridge.

*(At the edge of an outcrop,
an old rope bridge, in a
state of disrepair, suspends
over the ravine. Carter
approaches the bridge and
gingerly places his left foot
on the first plank and it
breaks. The moon peeps out
from behind some clouds just
for a moment and lights up
the length of the bridge. It
looks to be at least 200ft
long.)*

CARTER

I'm not going over that. Half the
boards are missing and the ropes are
as rotten as the gills on an old
Milk-cap mushroom. That's Manila
rope that is. Wouldn't trust that to
tie a dog to a post. It's alright
when it's new, but look at it. I bet
the last time someone walked across
this bridge Shakespeare was writing
'Romeo and Juliet'.

(Winslow walks over to the

bridge and wobbles a post.)

                    WINSLOW
Does seem a bit rickety.

          *(London walks over to Carter
          and Winslow.)*

                    LONDON
Don't remember seeing this on the
map. Better check to see if we're
going the right way...

          *(London pulls out the map and
          starts to look at the route.)*

...Doesn't seem to be any mention of
a bridge...

          *(London runs his finger along
          the map.)*

...Hold this light Winslow, there's a
good chap...

          (Winslow takes the light.)

...According to this...

          *(London looks off into the
          distance at two peaks on
          either side of the bridge.)*

...That hill over there is our
rendezvous point. Which means, we

are going to have to cross this
bridge.

> (London *folds up the map and
> puts it back into his tunic.*)

What time is it Winslow?

> (*Winslow checks his watch.*)

WINSLOW
Ten past eight, I mean twenty ten.

LONDON
That gives us 50 minutes to make it
in time. C'mon everyone. We're
moving on.

CARTER
I told you, I'm not going over that
bleedin' bridge.

> (*From the mountain range
> above, the whoop and ping of
> a rocket launcher can be
> heard.*)

LONDON
Take cover!...

> (*They all run towards some
> nearby pine trees as a
> bombardment of small rockets
> explode all around them.*)

...Get ready to run for it after
their next assault...

          (The drone of whirring blades
          begin to reverberate along
          the valley.)

...What's that noise?

               CAVENDISH
Oh, no! That's the HK-8 Blade
Dissector revving up.

               LONDON
What's that?

               CAVENDISH
Death by spinning blades. Eight of
them to be precise - 1 metre in
diameter.

               LONDON
What! That's monstrous.

               CAVENDISH
If you are going to cross that
bridge, now's the time.

               LONDON
Run for it lads!

          (London holds up the torch
          and begins running for the

*bridge. Another bombardment
of rockets explodes and
lights up the area.
Cartwright, Cavendish,
Winslow, Pilkington, and
reluctantly Carter, follow
suit. Behind them the forest
of small pine trees is
destroyed by the HK-8 Blade
Dissector and the area bursts
into flames. On the bridge,
ropes snap and planks break
as our gang of misfits sail
across at breakneck speed.
On the other side of the
bridge they all collapse on
the ground.)*

                    CARTER
I don't believe it, we made it
across...

          *(At that moment the bridge
          starts to fall apart, ropes
          snap and planks fall.
          Seconds later it totally
          collapses. Carter gets up to
          look at the falling bridge
          then looks back at London.)*

...There you are. I told you that
bridge wasn't safe.

                    LONDON
Well at least we made it across, and

I don't suppose the Russians will be able to follow. We should be in the clear now. I suggest we get moving, we still have a hill to climb.

> *(After a fast march up the hill, London and his group of ex-SAS soldiers reach the rendezvous point with 5 minutes to spare.)*

CARTWRIGHT
My legs are like jelly, I need a seat.

LONDON
Take one, you've earned a rest. That's it lads we've made it...

> *(In the distance the sound of a helicopter can be heard.)*

...Listen chaps, that's our ride.

> *(The sound of the helicopter gets closer and flies overhead straight past them.)*

CARTER
Where's he going?

LONDON
What's that chap doing, he's going the wrong way.

*(The helicopter flies over
the ravine and lands on the
hilltop on the other side.)*

CAVENDISH
What's going on?

LONDON
Chap must be mad. He's gone to the
wrong hill...

*(London pulls out his map
again and looks at it and
begins to twist it around.)*

Ah!

CAVENDISH
Ah! What does that mean?

LONDON
It means I looked at the map upside
down. I told you that bridge wasn't
on our route, I knew something was
amiss.

CAVENDISH
You stupid plonker, you can't even
read a map. We were right there.

LONDON
Winslow, hold up that light and wave

it about. Perhaps they'll see us.

> *(Winslow starts to wave the valve around and it slips off the rod and smashes on the ground.)*

CAVENDISH
You dozy Muppet, now we don't even have a light...

> *(From across the ravine, the Russians fire heavy artillery towards the helicopter and a barrage of missiles pepper the hillside. Several explosions occur and flames leap into the night sky, illuminating the area. Cavendish looks on with concern and interest, then, from within the fire, he sees the helicopter's burnt out metal frame.)*

...That figures.

WINSLOW
What are we going to do now?

LONDON
Get some rest, they won't be looking for us anymore. Might as well get some sleep.

                    WINSLOW
But we've got no kit and It's a bit
cold on this hill!

                    LONDON
Well I can't help that Winslow, we'll
just have to rough it...

        *(London looks over to a small
        clump of trees south of their
        position.)*

...Look, there are some trees down
the hill a bit. We'll bed down for
the night amongst them.

                    WINSLOW
Well, I suppose it's better than
nothing.

                    LONDON
Yes, it is. Now, get moving!

Scene fades.

ACT 4, SCENE 6

On planet EgÁs, Sir Daot enters the tomb of King KÁnTdiE and the Great Council of Arkanazak. Inside the vault, he sees Nelson hiding behind a large metal box and Tac, Eeb and MacTavish studying what looks to be a computer keyboard and monitor. They are examining their new device with great interest and resemble the mannerisms of inquisitive apes.

                    SIR GORF DAOT
Ah, Tac, there you are...

          (Sir Daot walks inside and
          joins the group. He looks
          around in awe.)

...Why, this chamber is vast. I never would have imagined we would find something like this. It's all quite bewildering. Any idea what all this stuff is Tac?

                    TAC
Well, I have to say Sir Daot, that I am at a complete loss. We've been looking at this box for the last five minutes and can't make anything of it.

                    SIR GORF DAOT
What about the Council?

                         TAC
They are through the back. Never
thought it would be such a grand
affair. Not much left of them I'm
afraid, but they are all there.

                    SIR GORF DAOT
Let's go and have a look.

          *(They start to walk through
          to the next room.)*

                         TAC
I take it you got my message about
absolute secrecy for the time being?

                    SIR GORF DAOT
Yes, but a little late I fear.

                         TAC
What do you mean, sir?

                    SIR GORF DAOT
Look, it's like this...

          *(Sir Gorf Daot stops walking
          and faces Tac.)*

...I have informed the Daily EgÁs and
have sent for a camera crew and

reporters. I contacted Sir Riffak and Professor Rellim Retlaw and told them of our discovery.

                    TAC
Why did you do that? Didn't Nelson tell you about the possible ramifications a find of this magnitude might do to the stability of our planet. Debunking the sacred doctrines of many religious factions and informing the masses about this chamber could cause mayhem. This is absolute proof that a more advanced civilisation lived on our planet thousands of years ago, long before the sacred scrolls were ever written. This discovery could pull apart the very fabric of our world and start a global war, it could even bring about the downfall of our planet as we know it.

        *(Sir Daot reaches for his
        pipe.)*

                SIR GORF DAOT
Good grief! I never thought about any ramifications. If only Nelson had tried a little harder to inform me.

        *(Nelson appears from behind a
        computer console.)*

NELSON
Well, it's come to that has it.
Blaming Nelson already are we. I
tried to tell him, but he wasn't
havin' it. As soon as I'd mentioned
you'd found the vault, he was off as
quick as a flash shouting it out to
everyone.

SIR GORF DAOT
It wasn't quite like that.

NELSON
Wasn't it. Then why is everyone up
there eating all the food and getting
drunk?...

     (Nelson points to the
     ceiling.)

...The time we get back to the
surface, they'll all be out of their
faces and fast asleep. All our
rations will be gone and there won't
even be a bit of bread and cheese for
us.

SIR GORF DAOT
The chap's exaggerating Tac. I told
everyone to have the rest of the day
off and get some food and drink. I
didn't tell them to eat and drink
everything we have.

(Tac looks towards Eeb.)

TAC

Eeb? Take Nelson and get up top and take charge of the situation. Tell them...

(Tac thinks for a moment.)

...Tell them we have found the tomb of *Lord Possyp the Great* and not The Great Council of Arkanazak and that they should resume work later this afternoon...

(Tac turns to Sir Daot.)

...Now, Sir Daot. How did you go about informing the media, Sir Riffak and Professor Rellim Retlaw?

(Sir Daot puffs on his pipe.)

SIR GORF DAOT

I sent a runner into town about 15 minutes ago, a young fellow with a funny toe and a limp.

TAC

That would be young EfÁrrig. Broke his toe a couple of days ago at *Blind Man's Ridge*. He was looking for some edible plants for chef Chief and got his foot stuck between two rocks.

Poor little blighter could hardly
walk when I last saw him. Are you
sure this is the boy you sent into
town?

                SIR GORF DAOT
Why yes. I thought he seemed quite
sprightly even with his injury.

                    TAC
Really? Well, this might be in our
favour. Right Eeb, as I said, take
Nelson up top and tell them about the
mix up and send someone to catch up
with that boy and stop him from
reaching town.

                    EEB
Very good, sir. C'mon Nelson, let's
get going.

        (Eeb and Nelson leave the
        vault and head back up top.
        Over by another console,
        MacTavish has found a
        flashing red button.)

                 MACTAVISH
Tac? Will ye take a keek at this,
there is a light flashing.

        (Tac and Sir Daot step around
        a few skeletons of machine
        operators and walk over to

where MacTavish stands.)

                    TAC
What do we have here?

              SIR GORF DAOT
What do you think it means Tac?

                    TAC
Not sure sir, but it seems absolutely
regular with its flashing. An on/off
every second.

                 MACTAVISH
How come we dinnae just press it?

     (Sir Daot looks at Tac.)

              SIR GORF DAOT
What's that chap saying?

                    TAC
He's saying to press it.

              SIR GORF DAOT
Oh, right. Here goes.

     *(Sir Daot motions past Tac
     and presses the button.)*

                    TAC
What have you done?

                    SIR GORF DAOT
Pressed the button. Why, wasn't I
suppose to?

                         TAC
We have no idea what it does, it
could be disastrous!

                    SIR GORF DAOT
What! Done the wrong thing again.
Why did you tell me to press it?

                         TAC
I didn't!

                    SIR GORF DAOT
Didn't you. Must be something wrong
with my hearing.

                    MACTAVISH
Take a keek, something's happening!

          (Inside the chamber, the
          dusty computer consoles start
          to flicker back to life. A
          low drone reverberates around
          the chamber and a high
          pitched chirping echoes off
          the walls. Reel to reel
          tapes begin to spin and huge
          cogs and gears crunch and
          grind back into activity.
          Sir Daot and Tac stand still
          as the chamber begins to

pulse and vibrate.)

                    TAC
Everything's coming back to life.
It's fantastic!

        (The chamber gets brighter
        and computer consoles flash a
        white cursor on a black
        screen. Above them a strange
        voice is heard.)

                   VOICE
DETÁ-VITCA ROTÁR-ENEG PUKCÁB. SMETSYS
Y-RAM-IRP G-NITUOR-ER.

                SIR GORF DAOT
Where is that voice coming from and
what's it saying?

                    TAC
Didn't quite understand everything.
It's sounds a bit like ancient
EgÁsian. From what I could make out,
something is being put in motion.

                SIR GORF DAOT
Is that good or bad?

        (Tac starts to shout over the
        noise, then everything goes
        quiet.)

                    TAC
TOO EARLY... Too early to say!

          (A slight purr of electricity
          permeates the chamber and the
          noise dissipates.)

               MACTAVISH
Ah, that's better. I couldnae hear
mysel' think.

          (From one of the consoles, a
          screen activates. Next to a
          flashing cursor, a question
          in ancient EgÁsian appears on
          the screen. Sir Gorf Daot
          walks over to the console and
          tries to read the words.)

               SIR GORF DAOT
...Egaugnal ruoy ni em ot kaeps...

          (Sir Daot taps his pipe on
          the corner of the console and
          some ash falls to the floor.)

Can you read this Tac? It's just a
load of old gibberish to me.

          (Tac walks over.)

                    TAC
Now let me see. Seems to be ancient
EgÁsian again. Right, I think I have

it. It reads, 'Speak to me in your
own language.' Yes, that's it.

                    SIR GORF DAOT
What shall we do?

                    TAC
I guess we better speak to it.

                    SIR GORF DAOT
What shall we say?

                    MACTAVISH
How come ye dinnae recite a poem?

                    SIR GORF DAOT
What's that?

                    TAC
MacTavish is suggesting we recite a
poem.

                    SIR GORF DAOT
A poem. That's not a bad idea. Do
you know any poems Tac?

                    TAC
Not really my bag, sir.

                    MACTAVISH
I ken a poem about a buxom wench that
falls in love wi' a dwarf.

                    TAC
I don't think that would be suitable
MacTavish, and It's probably best we
don't confuse this machine with your
unique way of speaking.

                 MACTAVISH
Fit way o' speaking is that?

        (From above a voice speaks.)

                   VOICE
Thank you. You may now give voice
commands in your own tongue.

              SIR GORF DAOT
Tac, it speaks our language.

                    TAC
It appears so.

                 MACTAVISH
Na it doesn't. Ah didnae hear any o'
my tongue in her voice.

                    TAC
Well, it probably dismissed it as
background noise.

                 MACTAVISH
Ye cheeky wee beggar. If ye weren't
who ye were, I wid give ye a batter
in the coupon.

142

SIR GORF DAOT
What's going on? What's that
MacTavish fellow saying?

TAC
Just a misunderstanding that's all...

(Tac looks at MacTavish.)

...Look MacTavish. I didn't mean any
offence, I could have worded it
differently. If it's all the same to
you, I would like to ask this thing a
question or two?

MACTAVISH
Ah, weel. I accept your apology.

TAC
Good...

*(Tac looks up to the
ceiling.)*

...Hello? I wondered, if it wasn't
too much trouble, could you possibly
tell us who you are?

VOICE
I am VACS, Voice Activated Computer
System.

SIR GORF DAOT
What's it saying?

                    TAC
Didn't understand all of it, but I
think it's name is VACS and it's an
acronym of sorts. VACS, could you
explain in simpler terms?

                   VACS
You ask me questions, I answer.

                    TAC
Right, I see. VACS, can you tell me
how old EgÁs is?

                   VACS
The planet EgÁs is 5 million 243
thousand years, 321 days, 14 hours
and 12 minutes old.

               SIR GORF DAOT
Great Fingledust the Third, that's
unbelievable. Millions of years old.
Just wait until Professor Retlaw
hears about this.

          (Sir Daot lights his pipe and
          has a puff. Tac looks to the
          ceiling again. MacTavish
          walks over to Tac.)

                    TAC
VACS, can you tell us what happened
here, how did everyone die?

                    VACS
5232 years ago, the life form known
as SAL entered the Mooron cave and
poisoned the water supply with a
plant called Hagweed.   The Mooron
Cave is the main water supply for
this installation. After 2 days,
everyone who drank the water died
suddenly and in great pain.

                    TAC
What about the Medallion of Life?
The hieroglyphs on the walls outside
the vault tell the story of a man who
drinks the water from Ra-eb's Claw
whilst holding the Medallion of Life.
The images suggest an eternal
existence. If this is so, why is
everyone dead?

                    VACS
The blue waters of Ra-eb's Claw only
work if you have the Medallion of
Life to activate the minerals inside
the water.

                    TAC
I see. Where is the medallion now?

                    VACS
SAL has it. After everyone was dead
or dying, she entered the vault, took
the medallion from King KÁnTdiE's
hand and left, closing the vault door

behind her.

                    SIR GORF DAOT
An eternal existence, well, I never.
I noticed those hieroglyphs when I
walked down the steps. I thought it
depicted the story of a baker and an
unsatisfied customer...

     (Sir Daot lights his pipe.)

...It's surprising how wrong one can
be.

                    TAC
Doesn't matter now, That SAL person
could have dumped the medallion
anywhere. And five thousand years is
a long time to unravel.

                    MACTAVISH
Aye, tis a pity. Eternal lee could
ha'e bin fine.

     *(Tac looks momentarily
     forlorn, then smiles. He
     looks to the ceiling and
     starts to speak.)*

                    TAC
VACS, do you know where the medallion
is now?

                    VACS
No, but there is a tracking device
within the medallion. If you
approach the screen on your left and
press the green button marked
'Ginmo', I will search the galaxy for
it. You may watch my search on the
screen.

          (Tac walks over to the screen
          and Sir Daot follows.)

               SIR GORF DAOT
What's happening Tac, what's that
thing going on about?

                    TAC
VACS is going to look for the
medallion throughout the galaxy.

               SIR GORF DAOT
Right, well I suppose that's going to
take a while. I'm going to look at
the Great Council over there and
smoke my pipe. Fascinating place
this, don't understand any of it, but
it's certainly fascinating.

                  MACTAVISH
If it's all the same tae ye, I think
I will gang up tap and see if there
is any food left.

                    TAC
Yes, by all means MacTavish, but
remember, don't tell anyone what
you've seen down here.

                 MACTAVISH
Secrecy is my middle name, see ye
after.

          (MacTavish leaves and Tac
          looks at the computer screen.
          On the screen, planets and
          constellations go whizzing
          by. After a few seconds, the
          images stop on a blue planet
          that is mostly made up of
          water.)

                    VACS
The Medallion of Life has been
located on a planet called Earth.

          (Tac looks to the ceiling.)

                    TAC
Earth? Never heard of that before.
How far is that from EgÁs?

                    VACS
Earth is exactly 5.2 light-years from
EgÁs or 1.59433 Parsecs.

                    TAC
Oh, I see...

(Tac rubs his forehead.)

...And exactly, how far is a light-year?

                VACS
A light-year is precisely 5.9 trillion miles.

                TAC
Gosh, that's a bit of a ride for the old bike, don't think the legs could manage to pedal that far...

                VACS
The journey is possible in 3.25 days using the Red Neval.

                TAC
Red Neval, what's that?

                VACS
The Red Neval is a 6th series Starship in the A class.

        *(Sir Daot walks back over to
        Tac holding a one foot high
        gold statue of King KÁnTdiE
        in his hands.)*

                    SIR GORF DAOT
Look at this Tac, this should fetch a
pretty penny from ChÁzz at the pawn
shop?

        (Tac looks at Sir Daot and
        his statue.)

                       TAC
What?...

        (Tac looks at the statue.)

...Magnificent. Just look at the
detail. Is this King KÁnTdiE?

                    SIR GORF DAOT
I would say so. Found it at the
bottom of his throne. The delegates
have a similar statue, but not as
large.

                       TAC
This is an amazing find. Don't know
how I managed to miss this?

                    SIR GORF DAOT
It was covered in dust. Looked like
part of the throne at first...

        (Sir Daot lights his pipe.)

...Thought I'd try and snap a bit off
as a memento, something to take back

and show the boys at the club; but
then it just came away. As the dust
cleared, I could see some gold
peeping through. Gave it a quick rub
and well, you can see for yourself.

                    TAC
This is truly spectacular...

          (*Tac looks intently at the
          statue.*)

...And you say there are more?

                  SIR GORF DAOT
Yes, a whole pile of them.

                    TAC
A pile you say. That sounds like a
lot.

          (*Tac hands the statue back to
          Sir Daot.*)

                  SIR GORF DAOT
Anyhoo, how have you been getting on
with this medallion thingy?

                    TAC
Well, it's like this, sir. We've
found it, but it's quite a long
distance away. VACS is claiming she
has a ship that could get us there in
three days.

                    SIR GORF DAOT
Three days! That's excellent news.
What are we waiting for, a bit of sea
air will do me the world of good.
I'll need a change of clothes if
we're going on a cruise. Now, where
is this ship, on the coast somewhere
I'd imagine? Let's launch it and get
underway...

        *(Sir Daot becomes excited and
        dances around with the gold
        statue.)*

...Yippee, launch the ship!

                    VACS
Launching ship. Activating pilot KAL
for Journey. KAL Activated. Mission
- retrieval of the Medallion of Life.
Commencing countdown. 10. 9. 8.

        *(The vault starts to rumble
        and shake violently. A loud
        noise fills the chamber.)*

                    SIR GORF DAOT
What's happening?

        *(The chamber starts to fall
        apart. Metal and rock fall
        from the ceiling and king
        KÁnTdiE's chair starts to
        crumble.)*

                    TAC
The whole place is falling apart.
Let's get out of here.

          (Tac, Sir Daot and the statue
          of King KÁnTdiE exit the
          vault and make their way to
          the steps leading up to the
          surface. Inside the vault it
          continues to fall apart and
          collapse into itself.)

                    TAC
I think we better move a bit faster
up these steps Sir Daot.

               SIR GORF DAOT
Yes, not as young as I used to be.

          (Tac and Sir Daot reach the
          exit and collapse in a heap
          onto the hot sand. Outside,
          the workers are looking up at
          the cliff face of Ra-eb's
          Claw. Huge boulders are
          falling down into the pool of
          water below and the ridge
          above is now starting to move
          and twist violently. Eeb and
          Nelson emerge from a tent
          with a sandwich and a beer.)

                    EEB
What's happening there boyo?

NELSON
Bit of an EgÁsquake by the looks of
it. Perhaps we should move back a
bit?

        (EffÁrig walks out of the
        tent with several slices of
        meat in his hands.)

EFFÁRIG
What's going on there? Strangest
thing I ever did see, the way that
cliff face is moving, seems to be
something emerging.

        (A burst of rocks fly in all
        directions and the Red Neval
        spaceship takes to the skies.
        Tac and Sir Daot are now back
        at the camp and stand next to
        Eeb, Nelson and EffÁrig
        outside the tent.)

SIR GORF DAOT
What the blazes is that thing?

TAC
I think that was our ship, sir.

SIR GORF DAOT
Ship, but we're nowhere near the
coast? I thought you said we were
going on a sea cruise?

TAC
I think you'll find that you
mentioned a sea cruise, I merely said
ship. If you had let me finish
speaking, I would of added that the
item in question, the Medallion of
Life, was over 5.9 trillion miles
away on another planet.

SIR GORF DAOT
Ah, so no sea cruise then, what a
pity...

> *(Over by the steps leading
> down to the vault, the ground
> caves in and a big hole
> appears. The Red Neval
> spaceship hovers for a moment
> then disappears into the
> sky.)*

...Well at least I managed to salvage
something...

> *(Sir Daot looks at his statue
> with pride.)*

...This should raise enough money so
we can go and look for that other
fellow you spoke about.

TAC
Who might that be?

                    SIR GORF DAOT
Y'know, that Lord whatshisface the
great.

                         TAC
Lord Possyp?

                    SIR GORF DAOT
Yes, that's him.

                         TAC
Yes, well...

     *(Tac removes a pink pill from
     his box and swallows it.)*

...The thing is, I made him up.

                    SIR GORF DAOT
What, made him up? Well, that does
throw a different light on things...

     *(Sir Gorf Daot puffs his pipe
     and looks at the statue.)*

...Still, it'll make a fine centre
piece for the dining table and an
interesting story for the
grandchildren.

     (Eeb walks over to Tac.)

                    EEB
What are we going to do now boyo?

                    TAC
Pack everything up and go home I
suppose.

                    EEB
Go home? After we've sweated our
socks off searching for that stupid
Council of yours and you had us
running round in circles for weeks.
Go home?...

     (Eeb grabs a shovel from the
     tent.)

...There's treasure here boyo. It
might be buried under a ton of sand,
but it'll be worth the dig...

     (The rock face begins to
     crumble and collapses over
     the entrance to the vault.)

...What now?...

     (Eeb looks at Sir Daot and
     Tac.)

...The next time you two decide to go
walking in the desert in search of
ancient ruins and the answer to
everything, don't look me up. My
mother said this was a waste of time

and she was right.

> (Eeb walks off over a dune
> muttering to himself.)

                    SIR GORF DAOT
Where's that fool going to now?

                    TAC
Don't know, sir...

> (The cliff face begins to
> crumble again revealing a
> large chamber with
> spaceships, aircraft and
> advanced technology.)

...Well, that's a turn up for the
books!

                    SIR GORF DAOT
Looks like we're staying after all.
It would seem the adventure is just
beginning.

                    TAC
Yes. Always did prefer the beginning
to the end, the end is so final!

> (Eeb walks back to the camp
> with a smile on his face and
> looks at Sir Daot.)

                    EEB
Are you seeing this Boyo? Looks like
a lot of good stuff in there,
priceless I would say!

Scene fades.

ACT 4, SCENE 7

7.02am. Saturday 18th October, 2025.
Inside Penachy Jail House, Felix
Botkin is informed of the usual
security protocols before he is taken
to Prime Minister Kantcoughsky's cell.
Felix Botkin is 52 years old and has
been a contractual lawyer for Prime
Minister Kantcoughsky for the last 25
years. He is bald on top with grey
hair at the sides and is short and
fat. He is wearing a dark blue suit
with white stripes and a pair of light
brown spectacles hang low on his nose.
He is also wearing odd shoes - one is
brown and one is black. Under his
left arm he carries a broken
briefcase. He is escorted into
Kantcoughsky's cell by a guard.

                    FELIX
Thank you, you may leave us now.

     (The guard walks outside and
     relocks the cell door.)

               P.M. KANTCOUGHSKY
Felix my old friend, it is good of
you to come so soon.

                    FELIX
That is alright, the wife pushed me
out of the house as soon as the K.G.B

turned up on our doorstep.

                    P.M. KANTCOUGHSKY
Take a seat Felix...

          *(Felix sits opposite
          Kantcoughsky on another bed -
          the bed is empty.)*

...How is Alina?

                    FELIX
She is stressed just now. My son
Felix Jr. is getting married in two
days time. She is concerned about
her dress, she thinks the sleeves are
too short. I tried to tell her they
reach her wrists, but she is worried
her arms will look too long in the
wedding photographs...

          *(Felix is a little nervous
          and is fumbling with his
          briefcase.)*

...I keep telling her everyone will
be looking at the bride, not the
mother-in-law.

                    P.M. KANTCOUGHSKY
Women always get worked up over these
things, she will be fine when the day
has passed.

                    FELIX
I'm sure you are right...

          (*Felix looks up at
          Kantcoughsky.*)

...But enough about me. How can I
help you?..

          (*Felix moves around on the
          bed to find a soft spot
          without a sharp spring.*)

...You know I am not a trial lawyer,
what has happened to Malovik, he
should be representing you?

              P.M. KANTCOUGHSKY
He has broken his leg, and his ties
with me. He has made a declaration
to the K.G.B that he no longer wishes
to be my lawyer. I believe this was
under some duress, but even so, he
has jumped ship.

                    FELIX
Mmm, I see, but I don't know what I
can do for you. It looks like you
will need a pretty good defence
lawyer to make a strong winning
case...

          (*Felix fumbles with his case
          again.*)

...That episode with Olga and the
pizza in front of the cameras is
pretty compelling evidence against
you.

                    P.M. KANTCOUGHSKY
Felix, be quiet. I don't want you to
represent me in court, I would surely
lose.

                    FELIX
Then why am I here?

                    P.M. KANTCOUGHSKY
I need you to get something for me.
You have an account at the Bank of
Russia, yes?

                    FELIX
Yes?

                    P.M. KANTCOUGHSKY
Do you have a safety deposit box
there?

                    FELIX
Yes, but what has this got to do with
your case?

                    P.M. KANTCOUGHSKY
Everything. The K.G.B have the key
to my safety deposit box and there
is, let us say, information I'd

rather they did not know about. They
have to get a warrant to open that
box, which means they need a judge.
That will take a little time. I am
betting they won't be able to open
that box until this afternoon. I
need you to get to that box and take
out a gold storage disc and hide it
someplace safe.

(Felix is becoming agitated.)

FELIX
I don't think I can do that, that
would be an illegal act, I think they
call it perverting the course of
justice. If I was to get caught, I
would lose my license and probably go
to jail for 20 years or more. I know
we have been friends a long time and
you have been a good client, but I
can't take that sort of risk, my son
is getting married in two days time
and I need to be there, not sitting
in jail next to you.

P.M. KANTCOUGHSKY
If you don't do it, your son will be
sitting in jail next to me.

(Felix puts his case on the
floor, his knee is now
trembling.)

                    FELIX
What do you mean?

               P.M. KANTCOUGHSKY
How soon you have forgotten what
happened five years ago in a little
motel room in Kutov.

                    FELIX
He was cleared of all those charges!

               P.M. KANTCOUGHSKY
Yes, he was. Who do you think paid
certain officials to lose damning
evidence against him?

                    FELIX
What evidence? They never even found
the girls head.

               P.M. KANTCOUGHSKY
No, that is true. But there was
other evidence linking your son to
the crime.

                 FELIX BOTKIN
Like what?

               P.M. KANTCOUGHSKY
The plastic yellow duck with your
son's finger prints on it. The DNA
samples that proved your son had been
at the hotel the night of the murder.

Funny how that duck went missing
along with the samples of DNA...

   *(Kantcoughsky sits back and
   smiles at Felix.)*

...The storage disc in my safety
deposit box has details on the
location of this evidence. If the
K.G.B find that disc, your son will
have to answer some pretty awkward
questions. It would be a shame to
spoil his new wife's honeymoon...

   (Kantcoughsky leans forward.)

...Still, there is one consolation.

              FELIX
What is that?

         P.M. KANTCOUGHSKY
Your wife will not be concerned about
sleeve length of dress.

             FELIX
You are telling lies about my son. I
know nothing of these things. I
never heard about a plastic duck with
finger prints on it or any DNA that
wont missing?

         P.M. KANTCOUGHSKY
You will if the K.G.B get to that

safety deposit box before you do.

                    FELIX
It's impossible, I won't do it. Even
if I did decide to help you, how can
I open your box, you said the K.G.B
have the key. What am I suppose to
do, take a cordless drill into the
bank and bore out the lock.

              P.M. KANTCOUGHSKY
I have another key at my house...

        *(Kantcoughsky stands up and
        moves closer to Felix and
        becomes very animated and
        grabs him.)*

...Listen Felix, your son's life
depends on you helping me. Go to my
house now, you don't have time to
procrastinate anymore. My maid will
let you in - just tell her you are my
lawyer and you need some papers from
my office. Get into the office and
get the key. The key is in the desk
drawer, top left hand side in a tin
marked 'Imperial Mints'. Take the
key and get to the bank as soon as
possible. Go to box 5237 and open
it. Within the box, you will see a
pale blue bag with a gold disc inside
it. Take out the disc and put it in
your pocket. Once you have the disc,
hide it somewhere safe. Do this

Felix for all our sakes.

> (*Felix gets to his feet.*)

FELIX

I don't know what to do. I think you are a liar, but I am not sure. Why would you keep all that stuff?

P.M. KANTCOUGHSKY

For days like these my friend, when I need the help of an unwilling participant. You'll be surprised what can be accomplished if you have the right leverage against someone; it is a great motivator. Now, go Felix, time is of the essence. Come back here and see me tonight and let me know how you got on. I will have another job for you then...

> (*Felix calls the guard and waits by the cell door.*)

...Oh, and Felix?

> (*Felix turns around to face Kantcoughsky.*)

...Don't forget to give my regards to your wife.

Scene fades.

ACT 4, SCENE 8

8.05am. Saturday 18th October, 2025, the Okan Military Installation. Dmitry and Yuri are fast asleep when they are suddenly awoken by a commotion in the next cell. The Moon Man is screaming at the top of his voice.

                    DMITRY
What is happening?

            *(Yuri moves from his bed and
            goes over to the west wall.)*

                    YURI
Are you alright in there?

                    MOON MAN
Arrgghh, arrgghh. A rat, an enormous big rat just ran across my bed. Horrible brown thing with a long tail...

            *(The Moon Man starts to
            shout.)*

...Oh, let me out of here! Let me out of here! I've done nothing wrong, I was only having a laugh. Oh, help me someone!

YURI
Be quiet, you'll bring the guards.
Do you want to end up like Viktor?

(Dmitry gets to his feet.)

DMITRY
Yuri, Listen? The guards are coming.
Get back on your bed, quickly.

*(The Moon Man continues to
complain and shout. The
sound of metal doors clanging
in the corridor get closer
and the door to the Moon
Man's cell is opened.)*

MOON MAN
Oh, thank heaven you've come, I'd
rather die than be left alone in this
cell with that thing.

*(The Moon Man points to the
rat in the corner of the
cell. The guard takes out
his gun and shoots the rat
twice. He then closes the
door and leaves.)*

YURI
They have killed him. He was a pest
and deserved a smack in the face, but
I did not want him to die.

                    DMITRY
At least it was quick and he did not
suffer.

                    YURI
So, that makes it alright?

                    DMITRY
No, but it is something.

                    MOON MAN
Oh, I'm not dead. He just killed the
rat that's all...

        *(The Moon Man starts to
        laugh.)*

...You thought I was dead, that is
funny. For a minute there it sounded
like you cared...

        *(The Moon Man continues to
        laugh.)*

...Oh, you have made me laugh. To
think just a minute ago I was in
hysterics, now me sides are hurting
from laughing so much.

                    YURI
You idiot. You are laughing like
it's a game. Don't you realise they
are going to kill you for real. You
have escaped this time, but next time

you will be rat.

                MOON MAN
You had to go and spoil it, I was
enjoying meself there for a minute,
you big party pooper. Just as I was
getting used to my surroundings and
that strange smell of stale urine.

                DMITRY
Yuri, don't interact with him
anymore. He is obviously insane.

          (Outside in the corridor,
          voices can be heard and then
          Dmitry and Yuri's cell door
          is opened. Two armed guards
          walk in.)

                GUARD 1
You two, come with me, the General
wants to see you.

          (Yuri and Dmitry follow the
          guard outside of the cell.
          The guard handcuffs them
          together and they follow him
          along a decaying corridor.
          The paint is peeling off the
          walls and everywhere is damp
          and mouldy. They pass
          through several locked doors
          and enter a lift.   In the
          lift, the guard pushes a

button and the lift goes up.
It stops on level C and they
disembark.)

YURI
This is a bit different to our
accommodation on the lower decks...

(Level C is white and clean,
the air is fresh and the
temperature is a pleasant 25°
Celsius. The corridors are
long and spacious and
motorised carts pass by with
friendly looking people going
about their business.
Beethoven's 6th symphony is
being pumped out at an
acceptable 40dB and big
monitors cover the walls and
advertise popular holiday
destinations in Europe.)

...I hope this means we are getting
an upgrade.

DMITRY
That would be nice, but not likely.
The spilling of blood on a white
floor is more dramatic and is easier
to clean.

YURI
Dmitry, do you have to spoil the mood

and mention the spilling of blood, I
was just starting to feel a sense of
well being and the music is very
soothing.

                    DMITRY
Yes, it is. I can see the mop and
bucket, two lifeless corpses on a
stretcher and a man wiping down an
assortment of sharp metal instruments
as the music serenely glides into the
second movement...

          (The guard stops at a door,
          opens it, and motions them to
          walk in.)

...Well it was nice knowing you Yuri.

          (Through the door, Dmitry and
          Yuri enter a large room that
          is very bright and is snow
          white. The walls are white,
          the floor is while, and even
          the table and chairs that
          dominate the centre of the
          room are white. Above the
          table, a microphone hangs
          from the ceiling and sparkles
          in the brightness. A drinks
          machine is in the far right
          hand corner and to the left
          of them is a large mirror.
          They are shown to two seats
          that are facing the door and

they sit down. The guard
secures their handcuffed arms
to the middle of the table
via a protruding hook and
then stands at the back of
the room looking very
serious.)

DMITRY
Not quite the torture chamber I was
expecting, but perhaps the house
dentist carries his own tools.

(Yuri looks at Dmitry.)

YURI
Dmitry, I wish you would shut up,
this whole thing is very unsettling
and you are only making it worse.

DMITRY
I am sorry Yuri, you are right. I
will be quiet.

(Outside in the corridor two
voices can be heard through
the closed door.)

VOICE 1
...All in good time Vadim. I need to
interrogate them first and find out
what they know. Afterwards, I will
let you kill them...

(Dmitry and Yuri look at each other.)

...Now, go to the Penachy Jailhouse like I told you and dispose of our other problem. When you have done that, go to the warehouse and set fire to it.

                    VOICE 2
What about the woman?

                    VOICE 1
She is what we call collateral damage. She knows too much and can connect us to the other bombings. Now, remember what I told you. After you have placed the bombs, make sure Popov and Ivanov are inside the building before you blow it up...

(It goes quiet for a few seconds than the door opens to the interrogation room.)

...Now get going.

(For a brief moment, Yuri and Dmitry see a man with a burnt face. The man stares at both of them and draws his right index finger across his throat from left to right, then walks away. The man who was talking enters the room.

*He is dressed in military
attire and looks unsettlingly
happy.)*

                    GENERAL GERASIMOV
Ah, yes. The two troublesome
cosmonauts that refuse to die...

        *(General Gerasimov lights a
        big cigar and takes a puff.
        He keeps the lighter in his
        hand.)*

...You two have managed to destroy 30
years of work...

        *(The General gets animated
        and excited in a bad way.)*

...30 years and billions of rubles.
Time and money that was spent
developing technology we no longer
need. An investment that has also
cost many lives...

        *(The General takes a puff on
        his cigar and paces the
        room.)*

...Hundreds of man hours spent
building a ship to dock with the
alien vessel. Countless efforts
trying to burn a hole in the Dome and
you two destroy it all in a matter of
minutes...

*(The General stops pacing and
looks at Dmitry and Yuri.)*

...Russia was about to become a new
super power in the world and be at
the cutting edge of fantastic
technological advancements. Things
we could never imagine or even dream
of. We would have had controlling
interests in hundreds of new
industries based on our discoveries.
We were about to enter a brave new
world...

*(The General takes a puff on
his cigar again.)*

...And you two clowns ruined it all,
just to save yourselves.   All of
that work gone in an instant -
Poof!...

*(The General blows on the
lighter flame and it goes
out. He puts the lighter
into his pocket.)*

...but, please, forgive my manners.
A man should know who his executioner
is before he is killed. I am General
Gerasimov...

*(The General takes a seat
opposite Yuri and Dmitry as
they look on with chagrin.)*

...Now, I am going to ask you some
questions about your time on board
The International Space Station and
the hours after its destruction. Is
that clear?

> *(General Gerasimov takes out*
> *a NR-40 army knife and gently*
> *pushes the blade into his*
> *left index finger until he*
> *draws blood.)*

                    DMITRY AND YURI
Yes, we understand.

                    GENERAL GERASIMOV
Good. First question - Who was the
first to discover the bombs on board
The International Space Station?

> *(Dmitry looks at Yuri.)*

                    YURI
That would have been Boris.

                    DMITRY
I think you mean Doris.

> *(Yuri thinks for a moment.)*

                    YURI
Yes Dmitry, you are right. Seems
like there is a lot of stuff to
remember these days...

(Yuri looks at the General.)

...Dmitry is right, Doris.

GENERAL GERASIMOV
Doris? I don't remember seeing
anyone called Doris on the ship's
manifest. It was very clear, two
Russians, two English and an American
called Hank. Another American by the
name of Grivil Morgiss was scheduled
to Join Hank Johnson on board the
Space Station, but the night before
his launch date he died in his
sleep...

> *(The General gets up and
> walks around to the back of
> the now empty chair and
> places his hands on it. He
> looks at Dmitry, then Yuri.)*

...They say it was SHC, Spontaneous
Human Combustion, but who knows how
these things start, faulty wiring, an
unattended cigarette, a log slipping
from an open fire...

> *(The General pauses for a
> moment, takes a puff of his
> cigar and looks towards
> them.)*

...Pardon me, I digress. So, as I

have said, there was no one called
Doris on the ship's manifest!

                    DMITRY
That's because she was a stowaway.
She was smuggled on to *Station*
without anyone knowing except Yuri.

(The General looks at Yuri.)

               GENERAL GERASIMOV
A stowaway, is that right?

                    YURI
Yes, I didn't want to leave her at
home, she gets scared and lonely by
herself, so I packed her into my
luggage and took her along with me.
I thought it would be a great
adventure for her.

               GENERAL GERASIMOV
You packed her into your luggage?

                    YURI
Yes, but it was alright, I left the
lid off of her container so she could
breathe.

               GENERAL GERASIMOV
You left the lid off of her
container, what did you transport her
in?

                    YURI
Oh, it was alright, she is quite used
to a plastic box for travelling.

          *(General Gerasimov looks
          bewildered.)*

          GENERAL GERASIMOV
Okay, forget about her travel
arrangements for a moment. When did
Doris tell you about the bombs?

                    YURI
She didn't!

          *(Yuri looks at Dmitry and
          then back at the General.)*

What do you mean she didn't? Then
how did you deactivate the bombs?

                    DMITRY
We didn't, Doris did.

          GENERAL GERASIMOV
Okay, how did Doris deactivate the
bombs?

                    YURI
She chewed through the wire. If I
remember, she was quite partial to
the orange one...

          (Yuri looks at Dmitry.)

...but she didn't find them all, one
still went off.

>(General Gerasimov looks
>puzzled and annoyed. He
>throws his knife into the
>table and points his finger
>at Yuri.)

GENERAL GERASIMOV
Arrgh, what is this rubbish you are
telling me, what was she, a mouse?

>(Yuri looks at Dmitry, then
>back at the General.)

YURI
Why yes, did we not make that clear?

GENERAL GERASIMOV
A mouse? You must take me for a
fool? You will tell me everything
you know or I will torture the both
of you for several days. It won't be
pretty and there will be a lot of
blood, but my methods always work.
Once you pull a few fingernails and
snap a few teeth, tongues become very
loose.

>(Yuri looks at Dmitry with
>great concern on his face and
>goes to speak, when another

*guard walks into the room
carrying a box and places it
on the table.)*

                    GUARD
Here is the box you asked for
General.

              GENERAL GERASIMOV
Good, at last it has arrived...

        *(The General smiles and looks
        at the box with great
        satisfaction.)*

...Did they recover the video camera
from the hotel?

                    GUARD
Yes. It was burnt, but the card
inside is in good condition and the
data seems undamaged.

        *(The guard goes into the box
        and takes out a video card
        from a plastic container and
        hands it to the General.)*

              GENERAL GERASIMOV
Did you look at the card?

                    GUARD
No, just the technician. Just like
you said.

                    GENERAL GERASIMOV
Good. Take him out and have him
shot. Thank you, you may leave...

          *(The General also looks at
          the other guard behind Dmitry
          and Yuri.)*

...You may leave also.

          *(The guards leave the room.
          The General walks over to the
          mirror and places the card
          into a thin slot in the wall.
          He turns to face Yuri and
          Dmitry.)*

...Now, we will see what really
happened on board that *Space Station*
of yours.

          *(Dmitry looks at the General
          and leans forward.)*

                    DMITRY
What do you have there?

                    GENERAL GERASIMOV
The card from your video camera you
handed to the press.

                    YURI
How do you know about that? We gave
that camera to the press only moments

before the hotel blew up?

(*The General looks annoyed,
but then smiles.*)

GENERAL GERASIMOV
I suppose there is no harm in telling
you. Prime Minister Kantcoughsky
telephoned an associate of ours and
informed him you were not dead and
that you had just handed the press a
video camera that might contain
information about the Dome and our
planet's true shape. If there was
any chance this was the case, we
needed to act fast to prevent that
film being shown.

DMITRY
Kantcoughsky! Is he behind
everything?

(*The General laughs.*)

Kantcoughsky? He is a fool, he knows
what we tell him. All he wants is to
win in the upcoming election and
marry your wife. It is only because
of this card he is still alive...

(*The General faces Dmitry and
smiles.*)

...The sight of you two at the Four
Seasons hotel must have made his

heart stop. On the phone, I thought
he was going to cry...

> (The General laughs for a
> moment and then his mood
> changes. Dmitry and Yuri
> look at each other with
> concern.)

...He is a cowardly blockhead with
the mind of a traffic warden and the
aptitude of a Gorilla taking a Zener
Card test. Enough about
Kantcoughsky.

                    DMITRY
Then who was it that put the bombs on
the *Space Station* and why?

                GENERAL GERASIMOV
I did. That is, I had someone else
do it. If there is time, I might
tell you the why. Now, let's look at
this film of yours.

> (The General turns around and
> speaks to the mirror.)

                GENERAL GERASIMOV
Mirror?

                    MIRROR
Yes General, what do you require?

GENERAL GERASIMOV
Play the video card, and play it in
order of date, starting with the
earliest first.

MIRROR
Thank you General. Accessing card.
Playing video file 1.

*(Dmitry and Yuri look on with
interest at the mirror. A
film begins to play. Yuri is
in a pet shop talking to the
assistant about a mouse.)*

YURI
I like the look of this one, it looks
like a panda. Is it a male?

SHOP ASSISTANT
Yes, this mouse is a male. It was
only shipped in yesterday, very
fresh.

(The General looks at Yuri.)

GENERAL GERASIMOV
What is this?

YURI
It is the day I bought Boris. The
shop keeper is very keen that I
should buy that particular mouse,
even a bit pushy. I now know why.

He lied about sex of mouse and that
she was pregnant. That is why she is
now called Doris.

                GENERAL GERASIMOV
Mirror? Play next file.

          (The screen goes blank and
          then a picture appears.
          Yuri's wife Ivanka is
          shouting at Yuri. He is at
          home in his back porch.)

                IVANKA
So, you are smoking again. I could
smell that in the living room. You
are a dirty little sneak. You told
me you were fetching some wood for
the fire, but then I remembered we
don't have a fire. I have proof now
on this camera. Wait until I tell
your mother.

                YURI
It is just a cigarette, let me be.
My job is stressful, I need it. My
mother does not need to know about
this...

                GENERAL GERASIMOV
Mirror? Pause file...

          (The General looks at Yuri
          and frowns and then looks

back at the mirror.)

...Mirror? Play all files for 8
seconds until I ask you to stop.

                    MIRROR
Playing first file for 8 seconds.

        (The next film shows a door
        under the stairs for a few
        seconds. We hear Yuri's
        voice.)

                    YURI
Can I come out now, it must be an
hour?

        (The screen goes blank and
        the next file starts to play.
        Yuri is putting a tray of
        Pirozki pies in the back of a
        van.)

                    YURI
Thank you for the pies, I will enjoy
them on the Station.

        (The next file plays. Yuri
        is speaking to a vicar and
        thanking him for some
        sausages.)

                    YURI
Thank you vicar. The sausages you

gave my mother were very tasty. I
will make sure I take these sausages
into space and eat them on the *Space
Station*.

                VICAR
Have a good trip Yuri, and thanks for
the tip...

                MIRROR
Playing next file.

     *(Yuri is at Mission Control
     packing his case. He is
     talking to the video camera.)*

          GENERAL GERASIMOV
Finally, we are getting somewhere.

                YURI
It is only 2 hours before launch, I
am packing my suitcase for trip to
Space Station.

     *(Yuri is seen placing various
     items into his case: pots and
     pans, sausages, contact
     lenses, a gas burner, lamb
     joints and his little tartan
     friend. The screen goes
     blank.)*

          GENERAL GERASIMOV
Mirror, what happened?

MIRROR
End of files.

GENERAL GERASIMOV
Mirror? Search for all files on the
disc.

MIRROR
All files have been played. Can I
help you with anything else General?

          *(The General becomes enraged
          and punches the screen - it
          breaks! General Gerasimov
          throws his cigar on the floor
          and jumps up and down on it.
          He shouts for the guard.
          Yuri and Dmitry look at each
          other and are visually in a
          state of panic. They start
          tugging at the hook on the
          table that holds them
          captive.)*

          GENERAL GERASIMOV
Guard! Guard! Get in here,
quick!...

          *(A guard rushes into the
          interrogation room.)*

...Go and get that other fellow, the
one dressed as a moon and bring him
to me.

                    GUARD
Yes, General.

          (The guard leaves.)

              GENERAL GERASIMOV
Now, we will get some answers out of
you. As soon as your friend gets
here, I will cut off his ears. After
that, I will gouge out his eyes. If
you are still not talking, I will
start on you.

          *(The General picks up his
          knife and waves it around.)*

                    YURI
Why don't you just ask us some
questions, we never said we wouldn't
answer them?

              GENERAL GERASIMOV
Because you are telling me useless
information.

                   DMITRY
We have been honest, Yuri did have a
pet mouse. You saw for yourself.

              GENERAL GERASIMOV
That might be so, but I know you will
lie to me when I ask you this next
question.

                    YURI
I never lie, ask my mother?

              GENERAL GERASIMOV
Okay, I will ask you this next
question, but it could cost your
friend his tongue...

     (The General paces.)

...My technician, who is now probably
floating in the Oka river, informed
me that the video camera, which I
have in my possession, was set to
automatically record any audio
communications. He also said that
there was a direct link to your
helmets. That means, that the video
recorder would constantly turn itself
on and off over the course of your
excursion in space. The card I have
here, should be full of files, it
should have had hours and hours of
audio and visual information...

     (He stops to look at Yuri and
     Dmitry.)

...but, as you can see, it is
practically empty. So, my question
to you both is, where are these
files?

     (Dmitry and Yuri look at each
     other for a moment, then Yuri

speaks.)

                    YURI
There aren't any!

              GENERAL GERASIMOV
What do you mean? Remember, I will
cut off your friends face.

                    YURI
Like I said, there aren't any. I
forgot to charge battery and it never
worked. You are right about the
settings, but the battery was flat.

              GENERAL GERASIMOV
Then why did you take it with you?

                    YURI
The card had the first pictures of me
buying Boris. I wanted them.

              GENERAL GERASIMOV
But why did you give it to the press?

                    YURI
I hadn't told Dmitry about the camera
and I knew he would get upset, so I
didn't tell him.

     (General Gerasimov gets
     agitated.)

GENERAL GERASIMOV
Okay, let's start again. Tell me
about the alien ship. Did you get
inside?

YURI
Yes, of course. You must know this,
you have our shuttle.

GENERAL GERASIMOV
What shuttle?

(Dmitry looks at Yuri.)

DMITRY
Yuri, shut up!

(The General walks closer to
Yuri.)

GENERAL GERASIMOV
No, don't shut up.

DMITRY
Look, what is going on here? We
thought you knew everything about our
return to Earth and you were just
getting some sort of sick twisted
enjoyment before you kill us.

(The General looks at
Dmitry.)

GENERAL GERASIMOV
Nothing could be further from the
truth...

       *(The General walks over to
       the east wall and pushes a
       button. A picture of the
       Space Station with the Earth
       below is shown.)*

...This is an image of the
International Space Station taken
exactly one week ago...

       *(The General pushes another
       button and the picture
       changes to show just black
       space.)*

...And this is an image of the same
location taken early this morning...

       *(The General turns to face
       Yuri and Dmitry.)*

...What I want to know is simple.
How are you two here? You should be
dead! How did you get back to Earth?

       *(Dmitry and Yuri look at each
       other.)*

                    YURI
I think Dmitry better tell you, I am
fed up with his disapproving looks.

GENERAL GERASIMOV
I could run my knife across his face
if that would help?

YURI
No! No, don't do that, I will tell
you what I know...

     (Yuri adjusts his positions.)

...I will tell you what happened
after the Space Station exploded. We
exited the Station and waited
outside. We could see only minor
damage had been done to our quarters,
so we returned. For the next few
hours...

GENERAL GERASIMOV
Yes, yes, I don't want a blow by blow
account. Tell me about the alien
spaceship, tell me what you saw, and
most importantly...

     (The General becomes very
     excited.)

...Did you recover the Medallion of
Life?

     (Dmitry and Yuri look at each
     other perplexed.)

YURI

What medallion?

*(The General gets agitated
again.)*

GENERAL GERASIMOV

What medallion? Do not come the
innocent with me...

*(The General looks at Dmitry
and then points at him.)*

...The Medallion of Life. It is a
solid gold 3 inch circle encrusted
with diamonds, emeralds, sapphires
and amethysts. Ring any bells?...

*(The General looks annoyed
and gazes towards Yuri.)*

...It's the reason for everything we
are doing here. If the ancient
scrolls turn out to be true, eternal
life is within our grasp...

*(The General looks excited
for a moment, then returns to
being annoyed. His gaze
fixes onto Dmitry.)*

...This one here knows what I am
talking about, he is no greenhorn. I
can see it in his eyes, he has seen
the medallion...

*(The general walks over to a
hidden cabinet and retrieves
a file.)*

...In this file, is your life Dmitry.
Unfortunately, some of your best
work is missing, but some information
is just too sensitive to commit to
paper...

*(The General throws the file
on the desk and pages and
pages of information
regarding Dmitry's life spill
out showing photographs of
dead people and various
locations around the world.)*

...Even so, there are pages and pages
of covert operations. Your
involvement with the KGB, countless
secret incursions behind enemy lines,
mission after mission. One file even
says you killed a village of children
just so you could obtain the
schematics to a revolutionary bagless
vacuum cleaner.

                    DMITRY
That is not true, the coordinates
given for the bombing of that plant
were wrong that is all...

(Dmitry looks agitated.)

...And it was not the schematics for a bagless vacuum cleaner. It was a top secret formula for eliminating unsavoury smells, a revolutionary odour neutraliser for a multitude of purposes, bathrooms, garbage cans, drains _and_ vacuum cleaners.

                 GENERAL GERASIMOV
So, my intelligence is a little off. It still remains that you gave out those coordinates and the bombs were dropped. I believe it was about this time you started drinking.

                      DMITRY
It was just a mistake, nobody was suppose to die. It was dark, I couldn't see properly. A 3 looks just like an 8 under candle light.

          (Yuri looks at the array of
          pictures and information on
          the desk.)

                       YURI
Dmitry, I knew you had been involved in some secret government activities over the years, but this seems almost impossible. How did you find the time?

                    DMITRY
You are looking at over 20 years work
Yuri, and the jobs were only 2 or 3
days away from home at a time. It
doesn't take long to steal
information from a filing cabinet or
plant a bug.

                     YURI
So, all these years as a Russian
cosmonaut have just been a cover for
your secret activities.

                    DMITRY
It is a great cover Yuri, I get
invited to dinners and functions all
around the world. What harm am I
doing if I gather information for the
motherland.

               GENERAL GERASIMOV
And, from what I have read of your
file, you were a great agent Dmitry -
in your day...

     (The General paces.)

...But then you continued to drink
heavily and forget what you were
doing, you became an embarrassment to
the agency. You couldn't be trusted
anymore. You gave vital information
about our military armament to the
Czechoslovakian Prime Minister

because you had been drinking
Daiquiri cocktails with him all
night. There is nothing worse than a
drunken spy with loose lips...

>   *(The General walks over to
>   the wall and takes out
>   another file.)*

...But don't feel too bad, your
friend is not so innocent.

                    YURI
...I told Dmitry everything about
myself. I have nothing to hide.

               GENERAL GERASIMOV
I do not think so, Yuri...

>   *(The General starts to look
>   at the file and takes a seat
>   opposite them.)*

...In this file is information even
you do not know, the lives you have
ruined, the people who have been
killed and the schemes you have run.

                    YURI
I have killed no one!

               GENERAL GERASIMOV
Directly, this is true, but
indirectly, many have died because of

your actions...

> *(The General shuffles through
> a few pages in Yuri's file.)*

...Ah, yes. Here it is. While we
are waiting on your moon friend to
arrive, I am going to tell you the
sad story of a little boy who not
only lost his mother in a tragic
accident, but also lost his father a
year later.

                  YURI
It seems like a sorrowful tale, but I
don't see what I have to do with such
things?

           GENERAL GERASIMOV
If you listen closely, you will find
out...

> *(The door opens and a faint
> breeze whistles through.
> Outside in the corridor the
> sound of music wafts into the
> interrogation room -
> Rodrigo's Concierto de
> Aranjuez is playing.)*

...Do not worry about the door, it
will close itself in a minute. The
lift sometimes causes a momentary
imbalance of air pressure and doors
get blown open. It is a sign your

friend is on his way here...

*(The General reads the file
and begins his story.)*

...Once, there was a young boy called
Vadim who lived alone with his father
in a small apartment complex in the
Kapotnya district of Moscow. One
day, the boy's father left the
apartment early in the morning to
catch a train to the other side of
Moscow to start a new job. Before he
left, he gave the boy his dead
Mother's wedding ring - it was a gold
ring in the shape of a broken heart.
His father wore a similar ring on his
finger. When the two rings were
placed together, they made a complete
heart. His father told him that he
could keep the ring to remember his
mother by and know that when the
rings were back together, his father
would be home. The boy waited for
his father to return later that day,
but he never saw him alive again.
The boy was being watched by a kindly
neighbour, so when his father did not
come back, the neighbour phoned the
police. Soon, the child welfare
department got involved, and when the
father could not be found, it had
been assumed the boy's father had
abandoned him due to the stress of
losing his wife a year earlier...

(*General Gerasimov flicks
through Yuri's file.*)

...The boy then spent several years
in different foster homes and became
a young reprobate who was constantly
in trouble with the law. Over the
years, he started to hate his father
for abandoning him. It ate away at
his very being like an incurable
cancer. His resentment became so
intolerable, that at the age of 16,
he stole some money from a cobblers
shop and ran away...

(*General Gerasimov gets to
his feet and lights a cigar.*)

...This is where our little story
really begins. That night, it was
very cold and a few flakes of snow
blew in the air. With no shelter,
Vadim looked around for somewhere to
sleep. He saw a light coming from an
old storm drain and he decided to
take a look. Inside the drain, an
old tramp sat cooking a rat over two
pillar candles. The tramp motioned
Vadim to enter the drain and he
did...

DMITRY
Let me guess, it was the boy's
father?

*(General Gerasimov stops
pacing and looks at Dmitry.)*

GENERAL GERASIMOV
...No, it was not. That would have
been a tale with a happy ending. I
told you at the start, this was a sad
tale and that he never saw his father
alive again.

DMITRY
Yes, forgive me, you did.

GENERAL GERASIMOV
... Now, where was I? Ah, yes. They
sat for a while, then the tramp
offered Vadim some old newspapers to
cover himself with to stay warm.
Vadim began placing the papers on his
body, when he suddenly recognised the
face of his father in one of the
articles. He grasped the paper in
his hands and began to read...

*(Dmitry starts to role his
eyes to Yuri to get him to
notice something, but Yuri is
listening to the story. The
General blows a puff of
smoke.)*

...The article said that a man by the
name of Jesus Rodriguez had died on a
train. It was believed he was a

Mexican farmer on a business trip
studying a rare strain of sweetcorn
called *Old Yeller*. At first, the
article did not make any sense, the
picture was definitely his father's,
but the name was wrong...

> *(Yuri starts to go red in the
> face. The General looks at
> Yuri.)*

...Are you alright Yuri, you look a
little red?

                    YURI
I am fine. I am a little warm.

              GENERAL GERASIMOV
Strange. With the door ajar, I feel
a little chilly...

> *(The General puffs on his
> cigar.)*

...So, Vadim went to sleep that night
thinking about the newspaper article
- *Why did his father have another
name? How could he find out the
truth?* In the morning, he looked at
the date and the name of the paper -
8th September 1995, *The Moscow Times*.
That was the day after his father had
died. So, his father had not
abandoned him but had died on a train
that day; but you already know that

don't you Yuri?

                    YURI
Yes, I believe I have made the
connection.

              GENERAL GERASIMOV
Then perhaps you can tell us how
Vadim's father ended up with false
identity papers on him?

                    YURI
It was a long time ago...

     (Yuri looks for inspiration.)

...I was young, I was in a fix. A
man had just died and I took the
opportunity to change my
circumstances. So, I swapped
identity papers with him.

              GENERAL GERASIMOV
But that doesn't make any sense. You
have never changed your name over the
years, you have always been Yuri
Chekov and Vadim's father's name was
Yuri Schekov. All you did was drop
the 'S' and steal his identity...

     *(The General stubs out his
     cigar on the side of the
     broken mirror.)*

...What I want to know is this. On
the day of Yuri Schekov's death, how
did he end up with identity papers
for a Jesus Rodriguez?

                    YURI
I bumped into a man on way to train
station and his wallet fell on floor.
He was in big hurry and did not
notice, so I kept his wallet. When I
took the other Yuri's wallet and
entrance papers for the academy, I
put other man's wallet on other
Yuri...

          (Yuri looks up at the
          General.)

...I wasn't thinking about the dead
guy, just myself. I knew I had to
get away from my problems, and it
seemed like a good idea at the time
to make the old Yuri disappear. I
didn't know man had a child...

          (Yuri pauses for a moment,
          looks down, then up.)

...What happened to Vadim after he
found out his father was dead?

               GENERAL GERASIMOV
Now you are interested? The next day
he made his way to the newspaper to
see if he could gather more

information about his father's death.
He was shown to the archive room
where he could see the original story
plus any related articles. Vadim
found a follow up piece where Jesus
Rodriguez's wife had identified Yuri
Schekov as being her deceased
husband. Vadim also discovered they
had shipped his father's body back to
the Rodriguez home farm near
Angostura in Mexico.

                    YURI
Why did she do that?

               GENERAL GERASIMOV
Why in deed? Vadim was now even more
confused. Some strange woman had
stolen his father's dead body and
taken it back to Mexico. It would be
several years before he could get the
money to go there and find out.
After working on a yacht as a
deckhand, he finally landed on the
western shores of Sinaloa in Mexico.
A few days later, he arrived at the
farm of Jesus Rodriguez. When he
approached the farm, he noticed a
family plot with a few headstones.
He walked among them and found a
grave with the words - *'Jesus
Rodriguez, 11th October 1952 - 7th
September 1995'*. He went to his car
and took out a shovel from the boot
and began to dig. The earth was

sandy and easy to move. After twenty
minutes he had hit a coffin. He
broke it open and inside laid the
dried up corpse of his father, still
wearing the same clothes he had on
the day he disappeared. On his left
hand he was wearing his wedding ring,
a half broken heart. Vadim sat there
and cried and asked for his father's
forgiveness...

*(Outside in the hall, voices
can be heard and a big
commotion is taking place
with lots of screaming.)*

...Excuse me a moment.

(The General walks outside.)

                    DMITRY
Yuri, wake up! That man is getting
to you. I have been trying to tell
you for the past five minutes to grab
that paper clip that is by your hand.
We can pick this lock and get out of
here.

                    YURI
What have I done Dmitry?

                    DMITRY
Listen, pass me the paper clip. I
will punch you in the face later on

if it will help heal your pain.

> (Yuri passes Dmitry the paper
> clip from the file on the
> table and Dmitry starts to
> work on the lock. Within
> seconds he is free.)

                    YURI
Dmitry, you are free.

                    DMITRY
Good, you noticed.

                    YURI
Quickly, look in box to see if laser
gun is there?

> (Dmitry rummages through the
> box and pulls out the laser
> gun and smiles. He walks
> back over to Yuri and starts
> to pick the lock on his
> handcuffs.)

                    DMITRY
Your lock is damaged, I will have to
use the laser gun.

                    YURI
No, don't do that. Wait until he is
in here and you can knock him out
first.

                    DMITRY
Yes, that sounds like a better idea.
I will take my seat and we will await
his return.

          (Dmitry takes his seat and
          puts the laser gun in his
          overall pocket.)

                    YURI
What was all that business about the
gold medallion. It sounded just like
the one I found on the dead Captain.

                    DMITRY
It all seemed very odd to me. Why
would he be interested in a trinket
that opens the door to a bridge that
doesn't exist anymore. That alien
ship is blown up, it would be like
keeping a key when you no longer have
the lock.

                    YURI
I have to admit that is something I
do.

                    DMITRY
What?

                    YURI
Keep a key when I no longer have
lock. I never use key again, I just
keep it. It must be something about

keys. I kept key to my first car.

                    DMITRY
Did you?...

          (Dmitry fiddles with his
          handcuffs and covers them
          with his cuff.)

...Perhaps it is valuable?

                    YURI
I don't think so, it was a Lada Vaz-
2101.

                    DMITRY
Not your car key, the medallion.

                    YURI
Oh, maybe?...

          (Outside in the corridor the
          screams continue and get
          louder.)

...That doesn't sound good.

                    DMITRY
No. No it doesn't.

Scene fades.

End of Part II

FIND OUT WHAT HAPPENS NEXT IN:

DOWNFALL - PART III

If you enjoyed this book and would like to be notified of my next release, please subscribe to the *News, Events and Much more* section of my website under the 'Contact' heading. If you have time, please rate and leave a review on Amazon to help increase awareness of this series. Many Thanks, Sam Lucas.

To see the complete collection of books in this series, *please go to:* **www.samlucasbooks.com**